Tony Edwards

A GENTLE WIND

Antony Rowe Publishing

*This book has been printed digitally and produced in a standard specification
in order to ensure its continuing availability*

Published by Antony Rowe Publishing in 2005
2 Whittle Drive
Highfield Industrial Estate
Eastbourne
East Sussex
BN23 6QT
England

ISBN 1-905200-10-2

Printed and bound by Antony Rowe Ltd, Eastbourne

In praise of Erik Sartie
and his haunting music.
1866 - 1925

To John.
Best Wishes

Author's Note
The characters in this story have never
existed anywhere other than in my
imagination. Any resemblance to
anyone living or dead is, therefore,
entirely coincidental

About the Author

A Gentle Wind is the second novel from former journalist Tony Edwards who has spent most of his professional life as a publicist, turning the media spotlight on a broad spectrum of products, people and places, starting with Carnaby Sreet in the 1960's.   His first novel, *Wilson Lacigam's Bentley*, was published in 2003 and focuses on how a modern day Messiah might compete for column inches in today's superficial world of celebrity glamour and glitz.

Never seek to tell thy love,
Love that never told can be;
For the gentle wind doth move
Silently, invisibly.

William Blake
Love's Secret

Chapter One

Roof down, volume up, the powder blue Porsche roared from the shadows of the hotel's underground car park into the afternoon sunshine like a heat-seeking missile. Left hand on the wheel, the other quickly twisting her long black hair into an elastic band, Angela Gannesh sliced an erratic path through the London traffic and headed for home, *'Jumping Jack Flash'* screaming in stereo at a clear blue sky.

Three hours earlier she'd handed the car keys to the doorman at the Carlton Tower, promising herself that Tim's invitation for a quick bite of lunch would be just that, and nothing more. But promises were meant to be broken, weren't they? No matter, with any luck she'd just about miss the rush hour and would be back in Surrey soon after five o'clock - plenty of time to shower, change, and maybe prepare dinner. Better still, maybe not prepare dinner; far too hot to cook. Perhaps she'd persuade Leo to give the new Italian place a try.

At the traffic lights she stared straight ahead, smiling appreciatively, avoiding eye contact with the gesticulating young man in the car on her right. It was the 'fancy a drink', raised hand and head slightly tilted back mime, with the 'what's your telephone number?' imaginary dialing with the index finger follow-up. All so infantile, so predictable but flattering, just the same, for a woman of 32 with a six year memory lapse. She checked her lipstick in the rear view mirror, quickly ejected Mick Jagger for Carly Simon, then foot down, away from the lights, still lingering on amber, down the A3 towards Guildford.

Leo was already home when she swung into the drive at 'Pelham Green Farm House' and parked beside the black Rolls Royce in front of the garage block. She casually ran her hand along the top of its elegant chrome radiator grill as she passed. It was stone cold. Pound-to-a-penny - or should it be 'one new

1971 pee', she wondered, now we'd been decimalised - Leo had come back at lunchtime. On hot summer days he sometimes took the afternoon off.

She walked slowly across the freshly mown lawn towards the side of the house, loitering to dead-head some roses on the way, self-consciously buttoning the jacket to the white trouser suit. A brief period of adjustment, a more sprightly step, head up, full smile, through the huge wrought iron gate, round to the back of the house where Leo, predictable, reliable Leo, would be laying by the pool.

Paddy spotted her from the shade of the willow, long grey fur flying, front paws jabbing painfully into the solar plexus, a cold, wet, fleeting donk on the cheek and off, back across the York stone terrace towards the pool, announcing the arrival of his mistress in a series of short, sharp barks and gangling bounds across the flower beds.

"Why do you let him do that?" Leo, laying awkwardly on a floral sun lounger, red track suit pants, white T-shirt, peered over the top of 'The Times'. "He's been digging in the gardener's muck pile. Feet must be filthy. You should stop him jumping up like that."

"Why don't you stop him, he's your dog and he's bigger than me?" She half-heartedly rubbed the front of her jacket with a tissue. Waste of time, the suit would have to be cleaned. Irish Wolfhounds had big feet.

Leo rose painfully from his poolside bed, hands kneading the small of his back, stomach thrust forward, some token knee bends, a few weary arm movements, feeble attempts at toe touching, instantly abandoned. He slipped off his clothes and collapsed backwards into the pool with a graceless splash.

She cringed, slid her hands firmly into her jacket pockets, handbag hanging casually from her wrist, turned her back on Leo's lumbering clumsiness and strolled back across the terrace towards the open doors which led to the lounge.

"Are you coming in darling?" Leo's face, wet silver grey hair plastered sparsely over his eyes, appeared briefly at the edge of the pool.

She turned and waved, shaking her head. "I think I'll take a quick shower."

Her girlfriends complained all the time about their husbands getting home late from work and not spending enough time with them. They didn't know when they were well off. Leo had only been late home once in ten years of marriage, when his car was towed-away from outside Cartier. She couldn't remember exactly what he'd bought her that time, he'd bought so much. Was it a ring, the emerald perhaps, or the tennis bracelet? Probably the ruby choker – much too flashy, too obvious. She rarely wore it.

The good news was he'd arrived home late, for once, after ten, giving her an evening to herself - alone. Bliss.

She crossed the lounge to a mellow brick inglenook fireplace, resolutely reaching up to wipe a tissue along the top of its brawny oak beam. No dust. Milly must have been. One more room re-captured from the builders and decorators.

The door to the dining room, on the opposite side of the hall, was wide open. A young man, long hair in a ponytail, white overalls, face speckled in white emulsion, sat precariously on a sagging plank, suspended between two step ladders, carefully painting around the beams on the ceiling. An older man, with a cheery round face and rosy cheeks, raised a crumpled flat cap as she poked her head around the door.

"We'll be through here very soon now madam. Probably tomorrow." He smiled broadly, tapping the side of a plastic bottle with a paint brush. "Boiled linseed oil. These old beams lap it up."

She nodded, smiled and backed politely out of the room, shutting the door behind her. Old oak beams might lap up boiled whatever it was, but the smell was quite disgusting.

3

Nine weeks of foul smells, noisy crashing and bashing, and dust - never ending, floating all over the house, dust - would soon be at an end and the original 16th century portion of the farm house would be the way she wanted it. Then, at last, work would start on the 1930's extension, the bit she hated. She'd promised herself, at the start, that nothing less than a complete transformation would do, something much more in keeping with the rest of the house.

Her white leather boots clattered noisily up the sweeping Jacobean staircase, sending echoes across the hall. It was nothing short of sacrilege, but she'd already decided to cover the rich oak steps in thick, scarlet carpet. The estate agent had said that such a magnificent turning staircase was a bit grand for a farm house and had almost certainly been pillaged from an Elizabethan manor house sometime in the distant past. It was big, very big, and probably one of the reasons why Leo had agreed to buy the house the year before. Big was important to Leo. Big cars, houses, boats, even dogs, were evidence of success, testimony to the big bank balance, conspicuous affluence, to be envied. And Leo needed to be envied.

She stopped abruptly at the top of the stairs, examining herself in the large gilt framed mirror across the landing, trying to catch a glimpse of Angie Newton. Apart from the boobs, big boobs, she was nowhere to be seen.

Gone without trace, the happily divorced, stoney broke, full of hope, Angie Newton, who signed-up with the Leo Gannesh model agency during the long hot summer of 1959, the year Harold McMillan famously assured her, and the rest of the country, that she'd 'never had it so good'.

But it wasn't 'so good' in bed-sit land. Pompous pledges from the deluded tenant of number 10 were not meant for the far-off banana republic of Earls Court yet, in less than six months, things started to look up. Mannequins, the classy clothes pegs of haute couture, were suddenly pensioned-off by a new generation of fashion designers who made wacky styles for dolly birds. Sophistication was out, sexy was in and long-legged fashion models, like Angie Newton, were suddenly in demand. But that was twelve years ago, in a different world.

She smiled as she slipped off her jacket and threw it carelessly across the bed, remembering the daily stream of girls who queued with her, like stick insects, on the stairs up to the tiny third floor flat, off the Fulham Road, which moonlighted as Leo's offices. Spidery eye lids, bloodless lips, kinky boots and mini-skirted thighs, portfolios full of photographs, carpet bags crammed with clothes, they waited patiently to receive the call to cat walks and cameras - and fees of three-guineas-an-hour.

For close on two years it had been fun, lots of fun, but as the birthplace of the bowler hat and rolled umbrella began a much publicised but absurd pretence to be 'Swinging London', Leo somehow managed to dismantle everything that had once been Angie Newton and slowly reassemble Angela Gannesh, decorative ornament, desirable escort, and trophy wife.

Paddy pranced into the room, across the bed and over to the window, barking at three disinterested horses in the field beyond the garden, head and paws above the window ledge like a glove puppet.

"How did he get in the bedroom?." Leo, directly below the window, drying himself with a towel, wore his irritated face – all screwed-up, mouth stretched wide over clenched teeth, eyes half closed, head shaking slowly from side to side. Lots of tuts and sighs.

She looked down at the bed and the smudgy pattern of Paddy's paws on the pale cream counterpane, coordinating perfectly with the front of her jacket. No problem, Milly would change the bed in the morning. Right now, she'd have a bath.

"Can I join you?"

Leo, naked, arms folded, leaned casually against the bathroom door, pink and white towels piled high on glass shelves to the right, a white marble vase with long-stemmed red roses over by the window.

She opened her eyes. He'd caught the sun on his chest, bright red. It looked painful.

"Help yourself, I was getting out anyway."

"Don't get out, stay and have a chat."

He stepped down into the pink marble bath which had caused so much trouble when it was installed three months earlier. Something to do with sunken baths taking lots of ceiling space from the room below – in this case, the garage. Head resting on the taps, at the opposite end of the bath, Leo stretched himself out, feet floating unpleasantly close to her face.

"Where've you been?"

She stood up, wrapped herself protectively in a towel, and slowly turned her back on the question. A casual look in the mirror above the two marble sinks. No visible signs of guilt.

"It's Thursday, where do you think I've been?"

"Thursday again? The weeks seem to go Sunday, Monday, Thursday, Tuesday, Thursday, Friday, Saturday, Thursday. You're always at Helen's these days."

"Don't exaggerate. I have lunch with my mother once a week – is that a problem now?"

Angela had grown quite used to the idea that she was a virtuoso liar, a talented cheat, proud of her skill to deceive, her ability to fabricate a fantasy. It had become a well honed art form – like acting, only for real. There were bound to be little fibs between a wife and a husband with a twenty three years age difference, it was only natural. She walked off, both hands clutching the towel close in false modesty, into the bedroom.

"Are we going out for dinner this evening?"

"I don't know, are we?"

"Yes please – to the new Italian restaurant. I think it's called San Antonio or Alfredo, something like that. Shall I book it?"

Leo didn't answer.

In 'Sulky', which Leo spoke fluently, a prolonged silence after a question meant 'No'. She picked up the telephone in the bedroom.

"Eight o'clock OK with you?"

"Whatever."

'Whatever', abbreviated 'Sulky' for 'No it's not OK with me but as you seem intent on doing it anyway, I've got nothing more to say,' was one of Leo's bad mood favourites. She ignored it and booked a table for two, at eight o'clock. What would Tim Thatcher be doing this evening, she wondered as she put down the 'phone. Together, in room 120, after lunch, he'd said he would work late, probably well into the evening, making up for the lost afternoon.

Room 120 had nothing to do with reality, 'A' & 'T', the 1st and 20th letters of the alphabet, all so childishly secret, exciting and completely stupid. With Tim, for a few fanciful hours, it was easy to pretend to be in love, act out the agony of a doomed romance, even fake some sort of bogus fidelity. But, as always, the real world paced impatiently up and down outside the room, waiting for the moment when she closed the door behind her and dropped swiftly back down to earth in the elevator.

Leo, in a white, monogrammed, towelling dressing gown, stood, silently, in front of the open wardrobe before picking out a pair of blue denim jeans and a sweat shirt with a large yellow 'Y' on the front.

"This Italian place - casual I assume?"

"Smart casual," she snapped back. "Wear your flannels and blazer."

Downstairs in the hall, the grandfather clock struck six. Tim wouldn't be working late, she knew that. Right now he'd

7

be locking the doors of Thatchers Estate Agents, before nipping upstairs for a shave and a change of shirt. Then he would be off, down the high street, headed for 'The Kings Oak' and a few quick sharpeners.

Tim drank too much. It was a well-worn joke that the personalised TT something or another number plate on his BMW stood for 'Tea Total', but he always managed to sound sober, talk sense. People liked Tim.

A visit to 'The Kings Oak', a good mile away, had been tagged-on to the tour of 'Pelham Green Farm House' when he first showed them round the property the year before, as if the former coaching inn was somehow included in the £25,000 price tag for the house. He took them there again, this time for dinner, the day they moved in. He'd probably be there this evening, fair, schoolboy hair flopping untidily across his forehead, entertaining the regulars with some well-spun yarns beginning; "This may seem incredible but…" or ending "..I swear that's the God's honest truth," and which nobody believed for a moment.

Although he'd successfully side-step the well-established laurels of success for a man of 34 - an extravagant house, matching wife, optional school fees, and a car which made a significant contribution to the national wealth of the OPEC oil-producing countries – Tim's quality rating at 'The Kings Oak' was still OTP [our type of people]. Certainly there had been a few intoxicated evenings when he'd narrowly missed relegation to NQOTP [not quite our type of people], but a booming property market meant that a successful estate agent could potentially aspire to the prized OTPBMS rating [our type of people, but more so].

The calm of the bedroom was shattered, without warning, by squealing trumpets, blasting their way upstairs. Hands covering her ears, elbows firmly on the dressing table, eyes closed, Angela sat, motionless, for a few painful moments, waiting for Leo to turn down the volume. Music for the hard of hearing, Herb Alpert and the Tijuana Brass, Leo's favourite, 'Spanish Flea'.

Carved oak panels, salvaged from a deconsecrated church, ready-made craftsmanship for the front of the bar which dominated a small candle-lit room, just off the lounge. Perched on a stool behind the hallowed structure, like a vicar in a pulpit, Leo carefully arranged two long flute Champagne glasses either side of a bottle of Perrier-Jouet, and emptied a packet of peanuts into a small, white porcelain bowl.

A heavy bouquet of expensive perfume wafted across the room slightly ahead of Angela as she made, purposefully, for the eight-track cassette player.

"Are you deaf?"

Tijuana trumpets instantly muted, Spanish fleas reduced to a background hum, she arranged herself on a stool in front of the bar, opened the small red bottle she'd been carrying, and began painting her finger nails.

Leo poured two glasses of Champagne, placed one in front of her and raised the other, jauntily, above his head.

"Well done Angela. You definitely can't see the join."

"What join?" she asked without looking up.

"The extension. It looks exactly like the real thing. I bet nobody could tell the difference."

She inspected the nails of her outstretched right hand before casually glancing around the room. Natural stone floor, bogus beams imbedded into white stucco plaster on the walls and ceiling, brand new oak, artificially distressed, stained, and waxed to resemble the rest of the 400 year old beams in the house.

"Well, I suppose it'll pass. At least it's more in keeping than the abysmal 1930's extension. They'd never permit it today."

"Peanut?" Leo pushed the bowl towards her.

9

"No thanks, my nails are still wet."

"But these are very special nuts." He grabbed a handful, head back, and emptied them into his mouth.

"Special? What's special, apart from a tendency to fall all over the floor?"

Leo waved the bowl in front of her. "See for yourself."

She looked down, irritated. Something sparkled through a pile of oily, salty peanuts.

"What is it?" She fumbled, coyly, in the bowl, wet finger nails forgotten, the frown quickly softening into a flirty smile.

"Goodness, it's not an it, it's a they."

She squealed, girlishly, and ran to the mirror in the hall, returning, moments later, adjusting the neckline of her floaty, flimsy, cream chiffon dress downwards, wearing a pair of diamond earrings.

"Oh Leo, they're beautiful. You're such a fool – diamonds in a bowl of peanuts. Whatever next?"

"Next, my angel, it's dinner at San Antonio or Alfredo. By the way, which is it?"

"It's neither, I'm afraid. It turned out to be another San altogether – San Marco." She blew a lethargic kiss across the room as she bent down to switch-off the eight-track, cassette quickly ejected and slipped, unseen, behind the curtain on the window ledge – half-way house on a one-way journey to the dustbin.

"San Marco it is then." Leo extinguished four chunky white candles with a brass snuffer. "I hope you know where it is because I haven't got a clue."

"You drive, I'll navigate," she said, returning to the hall mirror to fix her lipstick and take a closer look at the earrings. "It's just off the high street. Hurry up or we'll start without you."

The heat of the day lingered in the early evening air, now heavy with the scent of jasmine and the sweet smell of cut grass, the gentle touch of summer, her favourite time. She stopped, briefly, inside the front porch, completely still, eyes closed, deep breaths, a magic moment abruptly ended as Leo, keys in hand, quickly grabbed her arm and moved her, like an ornament, to one side while he locked the front door.

Paddy appeared at one of the bedroom windows as they drove off, barking noisily until the car reached the end of the long, gravel drive. Leo stopped, abruptly, just beyond the gates, adjusted heavy black rimmed glasses and peered, quizzically, back at the house through the rear window.

"How did that flaming hound get into the green room?"

"Must have left the door open." Angela sank back, impatiently, into the thick upholstered comfort of the beige leather front seat.

"I definitely closed the door. The decorators dumped some of their pots and pans in there before they left, so it's no place for a barmy dog."

He reversed quickly back up the drive, stopped outside the front door, and disappeared into the house. The distinctive high-pitched buzz of the burglar alarm being turned-off, in the hall, was followed by five minutes or more of complete silence before Leo returned wearing a different blazer.

She opened the car window and leaned out as he locked the front door behind him.

"Everything OK?"

Leo, smelling faintly of turpentine, a face like thunder, restarted the engine and headed back down the drive without a word. They'd nearly reached the high street before he finally spoke.

"I must have shut Paddy in the green room by mistake. Can't imagine how. I remember checking and he definitely wasn't in there."

Angela giggled, pinched the tip of her nose, sniffed. "Not sure about the new after-shave".

11

Leo gave her a withering look. "It's not funny. The mad bugger upset a bowl of thinners, full of dirty bloody paint brushes, and then jumped on me as I opened the bedroom door. Blazer's a write-off, looks like Joseph's technicolour dreamcoat."

She gave the back of his neck a reassuring rub. "Never mind, it was a bit old-fashioned anyway. They're all wearing double-breasted these days."

He'd calmed-down by the time they reached the restaurant, tucked away in a side street, sandwiched between a rather faded hairdressers and a florist shop. Small but snug, lots of plastic grape vines, pseudo wall paintings, fibre glass statues and columns. Leo called it 'Repro Roman'. A cursory glance around the room gave him the distinct impression that, with the possible exception of a party of four at a window table near the door, San Marco's regulars were NQOTP. He draped his jacket over the back of the chair and sat down.

"Welcome to San Marco dis heevening." The owner, short, slim and smiling, black hair greased back on a balding head and a slight gap between his two front teeth, produced two rolled-up scroll menus from under his arm

"My name issa Paul, same as de Pope," he announced, adjusting a red, white and green bow tie.

"Shouldn't it be Marco, same as the restaurant?" Leo asked casually, looking past him at the day's 'specials', chalked-up on a black board near the door.

"No. Why I wanna changer my name?" He shrugged, reached up for a wine list from a shelf behind them, then quickly zigzagged his way off between the candle-lit tables over to the kitchen, singing with gusto as he went.

Leo, confused, watched him disappear through a trellis of shiny plastic bougainvillaea. "I think I'm right in saying that conversation was complete nonsense."

"Sorry, wasn't really listening." Angela held the top of the scroll above her head with one hand, the other scrabbling to unroll it, downwards, into her lap. "This has to be the most uncomfortable menu I've ever tried to read."

"That doesn't make a lot of sense either." He tapped the back of the parchment, held high in front of him. "A menu can be unadventurous or unappetising. It can't possibly be uncomfortable."

"Well this one is, try it yourself." She let it spring back noisily into a roll and slapped it on the table.

"You know," he said, dipping some bread into a small dish of olive oil, "I'm damn sure Paddy wasn't in the green room when I closed the door. He wasn't even upstairs, he was in the garden."

"Well, there you are darling, he probably climbed up the wisteria and broke-in through the bedroom window. If cat burglars can do it, why not dogs?"

"Sarcasm's not very bloody constructive."

"Oh darling do we have to be constructive? Its terribly boring. If you must have a serious conversation this evening, could we agree on the style of décor for the extension. We really must get rid of that terrible 1930's feel, rip out the art deco fireplace in the lounge, the frosty glass panels, and make it much more farm housey."

Leo stared at her, elbows on the table, knuckles digging into his cheeks, bemused. "I hadn't really thought about it too much but I'd prefer a genuine 1930's extension to a mock Tudor mish-mash."

"But what about the bar? You said yourself, it looks fantastic, you can't see the join."

"Yes but that was our own little add-on for the 1970's, just a bit of fun. And we didn't deface authentic thirties architecture in the process."

She turned away, fluffed-up the sleeves of her dress, checked her ear-rings in the back of a desert spoon. "You can't deface 1930's architecture. Anything you do to it is bound to be an improvement on all those silly shapes. Anyway, leave it all to me," she said, turning back to face him. "I've found a wonderful tapestry curtain fabric in the shop near the bottom of Sloane Street, by the square, and Harrods has some fabulous bed linen in rich medieval colours."

Pope Paul's namesake returned, singing in a higher octave, waving a bottle of Amaroni Antinori which, after a minor skirmish with the cork, he poured with great ceremony into two balloon glasses.

Angela gently clinked her glass against Leo's. "To an enjoyable meal."

It wasn't. A better than average tiramisu, from a moderately well-stocked sweet trolley, was no compensation for the soft, wet, pappy prawns in the seafood salad and watery spaghetti with an anaemic, tasteless bolognaise sauce.

The bill, when it came, was presented on a red plate with three chocolate mints and a small card which read: "We hope you enjoyed your meal. Please tell your friends about San Marco." Red rag to a bull, instant umbrage, Leo hastily scribbled "We didn't & we will" on the bottom of the card and left it on the plate with exactly the right money. No tip.

"You can see why he didn't want his name over the door," he said, as they walked towards the car. "It wasn't cheap either."

"Tell you what," she said, hoisting the hem of her dress to her thighs and sliding, bottom first, into the driving seat, "I'll take you to 'The Kings Oak' for a nightcap."

"Are you sure that's a good idea?"

"Yes, of course. Why not?"

"Well, think about it. Rampaging dog, ruined jacket, lousy restaurant, rotten meal; not exactly been my evening so far has it?"

She grabbed his arm and whispered, slowly and

deliberately, into his ear. "What's more," she breathed, "you still stink of turpentine."

"There you are then. Do you think they'll even let me in for a night cap at 'The Kings Oak' smelling like a down-and-out meths drinker?"

"I'm sure they will if we ask them nicely." She quickly reversed back up the narrow one-way street, swung sharply around into the main road, and headed off in the direction of two large brandies.

The fading sun filled the twilight sky with a warm red glow as it slipped, slowly, behind the tall trees which edged the fields beyond the village, sending roof tops into silhouette around the green where only a handful of people still remained, languidly, on the grass. Two white ducks, wings flapping, protesting noisily, waddled to the safety of the pond, pursued by a small, yapping dog and a boy with a fishing net, watched by his parents, glasses in hand, sitting either side of a long wooden table in front of the pub.

Swirls of dust flew up around the car as Angela, both hands tightly gripping the steering wheel, tried to avoid potholes, rocks and rubble on the narrow track leading to Leo's personal parking space at the back.

"Why on earth you have to park here I'll never know." She stopped the car opposite two large waste bins, refusing to get out until the dust had completely settled. "Nobody's going to steal it."

"Perhaps not, but at least the kitchen staff can keep an eye on it for me. There's some funny people about these days."

Leo gave the radiator grill a half-hearted polish with his handkerchief, opened wide the glass panelled door which led into the back of the restaurant, through to the bar, and leaned lazily against the wall, hands on hips, waiting for her to catch up.

"Don't you think it would be nice to use the front door for a change, like everyone else," she said, stepping warily through the craggy, dilapidated remains of a once cobbled courtyard, heels stabbing into the powdery crevices, shoes potentially ruined. "I feel sure Giles and Paula would prefer it; my stilettos certainly would."

"But we're not like everyone else. We're virtually family, honorary Maxwells."

"If it means crossing uncharted territory to reach the back door, I'll happily relinquish my family ties and make for the relatively familiar terrain of the front entrance in future." She marched purposefully through the restaurant into the bar, Leo a few steps behind.

Paula Maxwell sat passively on a stool, near the till, behind the semi-circular bar which occupied an entire wall at the opposite end of the room to a huge red brick fireplace. She wore a black blindfold, tied in a pert little bow at the back of her head and stared up, unseeing, towards the tobacco-stained ceiling, legs crossed, hands clasped in her lap, large, round, gold bracelets around her wrists, earrings to match, waiting for the next question.

Her husband Giles, short, thick-set, recently 60, balanced his stocky frame on a beer crate in the centre of a group of regulars on the other side of the bar and waved a man's brown leather wallet above his round, bald head for everyone to see. The room became hushed.

Leo quietly arranged two stools at the far end of the bar and whispered to a young man with a tea towel over his shoulder who, grudgingly, produced two Napoleon brandies without speaking, never once taking his eyes off the wallet, now displayed for the benefit of an attentive audience on an upturned glass.

Giles Maxwell tapped the wallet three times before he spoke. "Please tell us, Paula, if you can, what object do I have in front of me?"

"I think it's something to do with money," she announced, hesitantly, after a brief pause, one hand flat on her forehead, the other reaching out, fingers spread wide, to the heavens, bracelets jangling down her arm. "It's a purse. No, I'm wrong - a purse is wrong – it's bigger - it's a wallet - a brown leather wallet."

Small bursts of applause rippled around the room, then slowly died away as Leo, rapping loudly on a metal tray with the back of his hand, issued a new challenge.

"Will Paula be able to tell us all what this is and what it cost?" He handed Giles a diamond earring and whispered something.

Angela turned away, embarrassed, back straight as a plank, facing the fireplace on the other side of the room. To the right, near the open window overlooking the green, Tim Thatcher in his favourite Windsor chair with the big red velvet cushion, friends grouped around him. He tweaked his left ear lobe playfully, smiled broadly and nodded towards Leo, now the centre of attention beside the beer crate. She raised one finger, then two together, made an O with her finger and thumb and blew a secret kiss from behind her brandy glass.

Paula Maxwell, head tilted to one side at an oddly unnatural angle, black blindfold firmly in place, motionless, looking as if she might have recently been taken-down from a nearby gallows, listened to her husband repeat the challenge and begin a slow and dramatic countdown from ten.

"It's an earring, diamonds" she called out excitedly, before he'd reached five. "One of a pair costing £900."

"Bloody fool." A voice from the doorway. "More money than sense." An elegant, elderly man, with a gold and blue badge on his blazer, placed an empty pint glass on the window ledge. "Bought a house for less than that a year or so ago." He left, shaking his head in disbelief.

Leo returned, triumphantly, to his brandy, earring held high like a trophy. "What did you think? Amazing eh?" he said, wiping it with his handkerchief before handing it back.

"I thought it was vulgar and brash." Angela took off the other earring and dropped them both into his top pocket. "You can wear them home if you like."

Paula, sight now fully restored, clutching a gin and tonic, nicotine-stained fingers combing through her short, grey hair, fluffed-up the narrow groove which always appeared across the back of her head when she wore a blindfold. She'd enjoyed maintenance-free hair since last year's holiday in France when, after a little soul searching, some gentle persuasion and a lot of flattery from a hairdresser called Pierre, she finally decided to end the pretence of being a blonde and go for the new elfin cut, short, straight, spikey and, above all, simple.

"Mwa mwa mwa." A volley of air kisses, blown carelessly across the bar, her eyes fixed on Angela's naked ears. "Don't I get to see the earrings then?" she said, lighting a cigarette.

Angela smiled politely, drank what was left of her brandy and slid the empty glass across the bar. "Pour me another Napoleon and I'll see what I can do."

"Make that two." Leo fumbled awkwardly in his top pocket. "You've obviously seen them already, of course, in your mind's eye, so to speak." He grinned broadly as he dropped the earrings, casually, into her hand. "How else could you possibly have known what they were?"

"You're such a terrible cynic Leo." She dangled them, one in each hand, next to her ears, twirled around a few times for the benefit of the regulars and called out to her husband at the other end of the bar. "Do you think they suit me?"

"They suit you fine. It's my pocket they don't suit." He turned away, rang the bell for last orders, forced two large gins and a vodka on to a tray full of frothing lagers and hurried outside to a table in the garden.

Paula pushed the earrings back across the bar with the tips

of her fingers, stone-faced, like a croupier passing chips to a gambler on a winning streak. "You're a very lucky lady Angela," she said. "Not many husbands give their wives such beautiful gifts?"

"Don't confuse gifts with investments," Angela said sharply. Her eyes flashed as she scooped up the earrings and slipped them back into Leo's top pocket. "Diamonds are not just a girl's best friend, they're quite good pals with the boys too. Ask Leo about their long-term investment potential."

Giles rang the bell again, louder and longer than before. "Come along now ladies and gentleman, drink up."

"Can I buy you two a quick one for the road?" Leo took a thick wad of cash, tightly wedged into a gold clasp, from his back pocket and slid it down the bar to Giles, hunched over the sink with a tea towel, drying glasses. "Take it out of that. And we'll have a couple more brandies."

"Just a quick one then or I'll lose my licence."

Leo, leaning forward, hands clasped tightly together in front of him, chin resting on his thumbs, stared thoughtfully into Paula's face. "What's the trick then?," he said eventually. "How did you know it was a pair of diamond earrings and how much they cost?"

She puffed smoke rings at the ceiling. "Psychic powers of course darling, what else could it be?"

"Oh come on Paula. Seriously, how do you do it?"

"I read minds. That's it." She looked across the room, focussed for a moment on nothing in particular, shrugged her shoulders, then slowly turned back to face him. "You know, you really must allow a little magic into your life."

"Magic's for crack pots and kids," he said with a sour smile. "Money's what matters."

Paula stubbed a half-smoked cigarette into an overflowing plastic ash tray. "That's because you don't believe in fairies," she said.

"Who doesn't believe in fairies?" Giles, towel draped over his arm, arrived with the drinks. He handed back the wad of notes and some small change. Leo tossed the coins into a glass bowl marked RSPCA.

"I was just saying," said Paula. "Everyone needs a little magic in their lives."

Leo swirled his brandy around then quickly emptied the glass in one large gulp. "And I was just saying that money, not magic, makes the world go round."

"I think I'd have to go along with Leo on this one," said Giles, tucking his shirt back into his trousers. "Let's face it, he's got a beautiful wife, a big house, a Rolls Royce and a thick wedge of money in his pocket. How much magic does one man need?"

Angela stood up abruptly. "I think it's probably high time we were off and out of your hair."

Leo outstretched his arm lazily in front of her. "A hand up for a tired old man if you will madam."

"Sorry, madam's much to tired herself." She leaned across the bar to Paula. "Don't forget you two are coming over to us for dinner on Saturday. We're christening the new dining table."

Leo rose unsteadily to his feet. "Hardly a new table. It's bloody 300 years old according to the auction house."

"We look forward to it," said Paula collecting up the glasses and moving off towards the sink before Leo could brag about the cost of 300 year old tables.

The damp chill in the night air was unexpected. Angela rubbed her arms while she waited for Leo to bring the car round to the front of 'The Kings Oak'. Across the green she saw Tim and some others walking together, in a huddle, beside the pond, before they disappeared into the narrow country lane which led to the high street. She wondered where they were going, what they would be doing and why Tim hadn't said goodnight.

Leo drew up in front of her, leaned across the seat and flung open the door. "Jump in quick," he said. "It's nippy out there." He took off his jacket and slipped it over her shoulders as she sat down. "Can't believe we'll need a blast from the heater after a day like today."

She looked left, up the lane, as they drove past. Tim and the others had gone.

"About Saturday," she said, patting Leo's knee. "Perhaps we should invite Tim what's-his-name to dinner as well. What do you think? He's usually quite amusing."

Leo nodded. "Nice enough sort of a bloke I suppose. We don't want odd numbers though so tell him to bring a partner."

She wondered why she felt uneasy and realised, suddenly and unexpectedly, that she was jealous. The thought of Tim with a partner was instantly painful, it hurt, and pain was never part of the plan. They'd agreed on a light-hearted fling for however long it might last, nothing more, no strings, no regrets, no worries and, above all, no heart ache and no pain. She decided she was just a bit tired and the niggles in the middle of her stomach would be gone by the morning. Yes, of course, then everything would be back to normal.

Her silent thoughts were soon shattered and the evening brought sharply, unpleasantly, back into focus, as Leo slapped the leather arm rests between them, boisterously, with the flat of his hand. "That's it," he shouted. "It's a code".

"What's a code?" she yawned.

"Paula's mind reading. I reckon Giles uses code words to describe the objects in his hand."

"Well there we are then," she said, closing her eyes and snuggling back into the seat. "Mystery solved."

Spotlights hidden high in the trees lit up the lawn as they turned into the drive and the front of the house came into view, bathed in a welcoming amber glow from four coach lamps, one either side of the porch and another two, much larger, jutting out from the top of the garage block.

Leo stopped the car just beyond the gates, switched off the headlights, and leaned forward over the steering wheel. "That's odd," he said, peering up at the house. "That's very bloody odd indeed."

"Out of petrol?" Angela asked lazily, cuddling her elbows. "Don't count on me for a push?"

"I'm sure I saw a light in one of the bedrooms," he said, squinting through the windscreen.

Angela opened the car window and poked her head out. "Well there's no light now."

"I can bloody well see that," he said angrily. "It went off as we came up the drive." He wiped the inside of the window with his shirt cuff. "You must have seen it. Looked like the green room."

"Probably the moon on the latticed windows," she said. "Either that or Paddy may have nipped-in there to do a bit of tidying up before you got home."

"I don't think that's funny," he said, rolling up his shirt sleeves, "We've probably got burglars and all can do is make stupid jokes."

"Oh Leo, don't be so dramatic. If we'd had burglars the alarm would have gone off."

"There's only one way to find out." He stretched over into the back of the car, reached for a large green golfing umbrella laying, rolled-up, across the seat, and set off up the drive, slamming the car door behind him.

He'd reached the front door, tossed the umbrella angrily into the corner of the porch and was on his way back down the drive before she realised that the jagged bulge which had been digging into her thigh through Leo's jacket pocket was a bunch of house keys. She rattled them out of the car window.

"Don't you think we've probably lost the element of

surprise," she said, dropping the keys into his hand. "Surely any self-respecting burglar would have scarpered by now."

She parked the car and waited as Leo, re-armed with the umbrella, opened the front door and disappeared into the house. Paddy, smelling of paint, front paws congealed with an oily coating of dark oak wood stain, tinged with random globules of white gloss, bounded out to greet her, then followed her, tail wagging, back into the hall.

"No sign of a break-in." Leo appeared over the banister for a moment then went off down the landing towards the green room. "Looks like you were right. Must have been the moon."

"We shan't all be murdered in our beds then," she said, starting up the stairs. "Although Paddy's paws look pretty lethal. One of us should dip his feet in paint stripper before he redecorates the house."

"I'll deal with him when I've cleaned up in here," he said, closing the bedroom door behind him.

A weak, silvery glow from a nearly-full moon filtered through the trees, sending shadows across the floor to where liquid gunge from the bowl of dirty paint brushes had already soaked into the pine floor boards, leaving a sludgy stain in the centre of the room and the sharp, sour smell of thinners.

Leo opened the windows to the cool night air and stood for a moment looking out into the darkness. A fresh breeze from beyond the garden sent a shiver across the back of his neck; a fleeting tingle of expectation and excitement which he hadn't felt since he was a small boy.

Chapter Two

For the first time in weeks there were more cheques than bills in the morning mail. Claudia Hamilton, looking like spun sugar in a fluffy pink polo neck sweater, pushed spikey, blonde hair out of her eyes, wedged it behind her ears, and set about arranging the post into four neat piles along the front of her desk.

Three tall arched windows presiding, church-like, over the main office on the first floor, gave her an uninterrupted view across rush-hour Bond Street over to the corner of Conduit Street where a black Rolls Royce had parked, two wheels on the kerb, to one side of the Westbury Hotel's narrow forecourt. A large, green umbrella, held close against the rain, appeared at the kerb on the opposite side of the road then dodged between the traffic across to the dress shop immediately below the model agency. Claudia half filled a mug with black coffee, no sugar, and left it on a wide, leather topped, desk in the adjoining room with a copy of 'The Times'.

Her day had started well, apart from problems with 'Kelly' who was now more than half an hour late for a nine o'clock fashion shoot in Covent Garden. No telephone call to explain or apologise, no response to the messages left on her answering machine. Nothing. 'Kelly' was living proof of Claudia's theory that models with made-up, pretentious names, were unreliable and Pauline Plank, 'Kelly's' real name, was probably the most unreliable girl on the agency books.

Leo Gannesh dabbed his face with a handkerchief, shook the wet from the bottom of his trouser legs and burst through the swing doors opposite the lift. He speared the metal tip of his rain-soaked umbrella into the dry, flaky soil of a well-polished rubber plant which stood, half way to the ceiling, in a red ceramic pot in the corner, sending a steady trickle of water, unseen, across the tiled floor towards the edge of a tall, bamboo reception counter.

The girl seated languorously behind it flicked, casually, through a glossy magazine, her head just visible above a row of different coloured 'phones, frizzy red hair bursting out from under a khaki cap with 'US Army', printed in yellow, across the front. "You'll kill that plant doing that," she said, eyes fixed on the 'Ask Glenda' page. "Bugger-up the roots you will."

"Oh, I'm fine thank you Sara," he whispered sarcastically. "Thank you for asking. And how are you today my sweet?"

Sara stared back, blankly, as he reached in front of her, snatched a small pile of telephone messages and disappeared into his office. "Perhaps you might find a gap in your busy schedule to ask Claudia if she would care to join me when she gets off the 'phone."

Claudia opened the last of the post, the 'phone wedged between her left ear and shoulder, listening, nodding in agreement to the irate photographer who'd called to say that 'Kelly' had now arrived, without the selection of shoes she'd been told to bring to the session and looking as if she hadn't slept for three weeks. He'd sent her away and would be charging the Leo Gannesh model agency for everyone's wasted time. She put the 'phone down quietly, perched on the edge of the desk, one foot swinging just above the floor, looking out at the rain, dispirited, let down.

The brief message she left on Pauline Plank's answering machine made her feel a bit better. "You're fired," she said. "Get yourself another agent." Then she hung up, hurriedly scooped up the post, and took it into the next door office.

Leo Gannesh slapped the newspaper headlines angrily with the back of his hand. "They're taking their bikini tops off on the French Riviera." He prodded the offending story with his finger then quickly turned the page and gave another back-hander to news that hot pants had been worn in the Royal

25

enclosure at Ascot. "Whatever happened to sophistication and style?" he said, throwing the newspaper across the desk in Claudia's general direction.

"They went out of fashion I suppose. Do you want to go through the post now or shall I come back later?"

He shook his head, pointed to her usual chair on the other side of the desk, then, leaning heavily back into his seat, swivelled round to face the wall and a portrait photograph of his wife in a polished wood frame.

"Send Angela some roses would you? A dozen, long stems, red. No note." Leo turned quickly back, placed his hands, palms down, flat on the desk, straightened his back, eyes focussed and ready for business. "So, what's new?" he said with an expectant smile.

"A few cheques in the post, not too many invoices, couple of booking confirmations, the usual advertising mailers and an invitation to a pro-Common Market seminar." Claudia set them out carefully in front of him, moved her chair closer to the desk, and sat down, legs crossed, clasping a note book tightly to her chest. "What are the roses for?" she asked.

"Statutory penalty for a rotten evening. It's twelve for a minor offence, more for serious crimes." Leo tapped the desk impatiently with the tips of his fingers. "Shall we get on?"

She slid back into the chair, fanning herself with a telephone bill, checked her notes for the day then let her eyes casually stray towards a brass desk lamp to her right before she spoke. "I've had to let Kelly go," she said.

Leo stood up slowly, expressionless, as if he hadn't heard, pushed his chair back, walked over to the window and opened it wide. The rain had stopped and Bond Street glistened in the weak sunlight. "Must be lots of pretty girls down there," he said, leaning out with both hands on the window sill. "Pretty, but far from perfect." He turned his head towards her, looking across his shoulder. "Young girls like Kelly are about as good as they get."

"And as bad," said Claudia, slapping her note book down on the desk. "We can't afford her kind of amateur dramatics."

"How old do you think I am?" Leo asked suddenly. He set his chin at an uneasy angle and waited for her reply.

"Never really thought about it," she said. "Why?"

"OK then how old do I look? Honestly." He stepped back from the window, smarmed down his hair with both hands, tweaked the Windsor knot in his dark blue striped tie.

Claudia folded her arms, relaxed back in the chair, studying the figure, posing awkwardly beside the desk and shrugged her shoulders. "I don't know," she said eventually. "Difficult to say. Fifty something?"

"Try sixty something. Sixty one to be exact, old enough to be Kelly's grandfather." Leo buttoned his jacket, smoothed the front down, tummy held in and turned to profile, one hand loosely touching the edge of the desk.

"So you're wearing well then," she said, standing up and pushing her chair back. "Look I don't want to appear rude, Leo, but I've got a pile of work. Can this wait?"

He clasped his hands together tightly and sighed, searching the floor for the right words. "Just tell me honestly Claudia, do I look silly, out of place? Am I too old?"

She stared at him for a moment then shook her head. "Too old for what?"

"To be messing about with young girls, in the glamour business." He turned away, checked his jacket pockets as if he'd lost something. "Do you see what I'm getting at? I mean, I've got a wife young enough to be my daughter and I've started to look as if I might be her father."

"Oh come on Leo," she said quietly. "You and Angela look great together."

"Ten years ago you may have been right." He flopped down in the swivel chair and swung round to face the portrait

27

on the wall. "But now I wonder. Sometimes I feel I'm part of the wrong generation."

Claudia smiled, collected her things and started across the room. "You're just a bit under the weather," she said as she shut the door.

He didn't like to be told he was 'under the weather'. For a start he didn't really know what it meant, 'under the weather'. What he felt was 'out of place'; had done for about a year, ever since they moved into 'Pelham Green Farm House'. But then he always felt like that when he moved house. It usually took six months to a year to really settle-in, get to know the place, feel at home.

Upstairs in the gents, on the second floor, a brutal white fluorescent light above the sink gave his face a pasty, anaemic pallor, highlighting a flabby jaw-line and casting dark shadows under his eyes. The fine, silver hairs on the top of his head vanished in the spiteful glow which penetrated through to his freckled scalp, giving an unwelcome preview of baldness yet to come. Leo Gannesh looked at himself from all angles in the mirror as he dried his hands with a paper towel and decided that fluorescent lighting was cruelly invented by a vindictive mortician who wanted us all to see just how we'll look when we've been dead for a week.

The veins on the back of his hands bulged through sun-tanned, parchment skin, like an embossed road map, as he gripped the banister on the way back down the stairs to the office. Bulbous veins, fuller and fatter than they used to be, definitely bluer, old people's hands. He fiddled awkwardly with his cuff links, eyes partially closed, trying to read the 'Reception' sign on the door at the end of the corridor. With his arm raised above his head the veins seemed almost to disappear. Without his glasses it was much the same with the sign at the end of the corridor; it all but disappeared.

Leo Gannesh had started to realise that the inevitable

process of growing older often involved a series of unpleasant contradictions. It was clear that as the ravages of time came sharply into focus, the rest of the world slipped slowly out of sight, reduced to little more than a foggy blur. Ironically even the hair on his head seemed to be falling out at roughly the same rate as strong, healthy hair grew up his nose, in his ears and god only knows where else.

Claudia, wearing a worried frown, poked her head round the door as Leo settled himself at his desk. "Shouldn't you be somewhere else?" she said, tapping a large yellow plastic watch on her wrist. "Eleven o'clock, Mr Silverman."

He opened the red desk diary in front of him and slapped his forehead twice with the flat of his hand. "Forgot all about it," he said wearily. "Where's Kingly Street anyway?"

"Just round the corner from Carnaby Street." She walked quickly over to a cupboard with folding, louvered doors which filled the wall opposite Leo's desk, carefully selected a handful of model cards and slipped them into a leather brief case which she placed next to the telephone on his desk. "Mr Silverman needs a dozen girls for the opening of his new 'Birds' boutique. Must be size eight and blonde. He thinks you should see what he's got in mind."

Leo nodded, picked up the brief case, waved his hand, weakly, as a token thank you and set off to look for a taxi.

'Birds' boutique was in turmoil when he arrived in Kingly Street at about twenty past eleven. A steady stream of workmen hurried between the shop and two large vans, back doors wide open, parked immediately outside. Inside painters, carpenters and electricians yelled to each other above the sound of blaring music from a radio precariously balanced on the top of a pile of rubble in the corner.

"Sorry about the mess." A man with a pudgey face, black cropped hair and a bushy moustache, appeared from nowhere through a gaping hole in the wall. He wore baggy brown trousers supported by a wide leather belt and red braces which clashed with an orange corduroy shirt. "I'm afraid we're a bit behind schedule," he said, gesturing to Leo to follow him through to the back of the shop where a small wooden table and two garden chairs served as a make-shift office. He pushed the smaller of two chairs towards Leo and sat down in the other.

"When are you due to open Mr Silverman?" said Leo, looking quickly around at the chaos.

"Next week". He smiled broadly. "And please call me Sammy, everybody does. Can I get you some tea?"

Leo glanced across at four dirty mugs, long since abandoned in the soggy mess of some used tea bags scattered on a rusting tin tray. "Not just now thank you Sammy. Perhaps later."

Sammy Silverman took some rolled-up plans from a grey filing cabinet and spread them across the table, using an ash tray and a sugar bowl to hold down the edges. "What do you think?" he asked proudly. "It's my daughter's idea. She's going to be an interior designer you know."

"Interesting," said Leo cautiously. "The shop front looks a bit like a jail. All those bars."

"Not a jail, a cage." Sammy Silverman reached impatiently for a second rolled-up sheet and smoothed it out across the table. "You see, it's a bird cage," he said, looking into Leo's face for a reaction.

Leo peered down at the drawings in disbelief. From what he could see Mr Silverman's shop would probably resemble a giant budgerigar cage; rows of shiny steel bars along the front and silver bars painted on light blue walls and curved ceiling inside. The clothes were to be hung on wooden perches and a large round mirror, suspended from a heavy gold chain, was planned as the focal point for the centre of the shop.

"It's certainly a very original concept," Leo said half-heartedly, nodding his head, smiling weakly. "Bold and original - and hugely inventive too," he added, quickly, hoping he'd said enough to satisfy Sammy Silverman's ego.

"Thank you. But, to me at least, it was obvious," said Silverman smugly. "Where would you expect to find beautiful birds? In a bird cage, of course, where else? So that's how come we've got a shop called 'Birds' which looks like a bird cage."

"And my models?" Leo asked, reaching into his briefcase. He spread the model cards across the table, on top of the drawings. "What do you want them to wear?"

"Canary yellow." Silverman slid his chair closer, one hand squeezing Leo's arm, the other pointing to an unseen tableau somewhere beyond the blank wall in front of them. "Bright yellow mini skirts, jeans, and hot pants. Everything in yellow." He gripped the arm tighter. "And they'll be swinging on perches, like birds - 'dolly birds'. What do you think? Will the press like it?"

Leo didn't answer. He hurriedly arranged the model cards in order of preference, his mind drifting nostalgically back to the Champagne openings of the haute couture salons; crystal chandeliers, plush velvet carpets, stately cat walks, satin drapes and, of course, the supreme elegance of the models.

"I think these girls would be best suited for the job," he said decisively. "Their rates are £10 an hour, minimum two hours booking."

Silverman's head waggled and bobbed. He looked disappointed. "£240 is a lot of money," he sighed. "I was thinking of maybe less."

"No problem Sammy, have maybe less models," said Leo sharply, scooping up some of the cards and dropping them back into the briefcase.

He smiled briefly, picturing the response from a mannequin if he'd asked her to swing on a perch in a budgerigar cage and

31

decided that he would never have asked a sophisticated woman to wear canary yellow hot pants in the first place. But a golden era of beautiful women had passed, replaced by a new generation of pretty girls.

"How many girls for £150," Silverman asked coyly.

"Seven and a half," said Leo. "But we don't do halves. You can have seven girls for £140 and spend the extra £10 on an insurance policy in case one of them falls off their perch."

They agreed, finally, on eight models at the going rate. Leo said his goodbyes, wished Sammy Silverman luck with his new shop and stepped carefully through the rubble, back into Kingly Street and relative normality. He stopped to brush the dust from his jacket, shined his shoes on the back of his trouser legs and then set off across Regent Street for a brisk walk back to the office, stopping off, briefly, to see a magazine editor in Hanover Square.

"Any messages?" he yelled as he swept through reception and into his office. Nobody answered. For as long as he could remember none of the girls ever managed to answer that simple question, not immediately anyway. Instead they slowly and grudgingly rummaged through their desks in a random search for elusive telephone message slips, somehow mislaid in a confusion of paper, like chickens raking through farmyard dust. Then they would wearily assure him that, as far as they could remember, there was nothing important and it could probably 'wait'.

Today, he decided, it probably couldn't 'wait' and stood, impatiently, in front of the reception desk, tapping his finger nails on the side of a red telephone. Sara finally handed over four pink message slips with a huge sigh. One of them, she admitted, might have been from the day before, from a doctor somebody. She didn't quite get the name, sounded foreign, but he didn't seem to be in any hurry for a reply. Claudia produced three more pink slips, unspeaking, before he returned to his office.

Doctor somebody had good news. The tests had shown that there was nothing wrong with his heart. In fact it was relatively sound for a man of his age. He should try to take more light exercise, drink less alcohol and avoid stressful situations.

He leaned back in the chair, telephone in his left hand, loosening his tie with the other. "Chance would be a fine thing," he chuckled. "My whole life is a stressful bloody situation, relieved only by a daily intake of alcohol."

"Then I can take no responsibility for the condition of your liver," said a soft, cheerful voice on the other end of the 'phone. "Just don't overdo it. Take it easy. You'll be good for quite a few thousand more miles."

Leo put down the 'phone, relieved, already feeling somehow fitter, less tired. Apart from a minor twinge in one of his front teeth, he had nothing specific to complain about.

The call to Angela was brief. She was on her way out; literally half way through the door. It was, of course, marvellous news but hadn't she already told him he was worrying about nothing. No time to talk now. They'd chat about it this evening. Had to dash. She put the 'phone down before he could ask her where she was going and what time she might be back.

He wondered if she'd received the roses. She hadn't mentioned them.

"Off for a quick bite of lunch," Claudia called out as she hurried through reception, past Leo's open door. "Won't be long."

"Get me a prawns and mayonnaise in brown bread, would you?" somebody shouted after her. "No lettuce."

Claudia gave a silent thumbs-up, hand raised above her head, without looking back, and disappeared through the swing doors.

A prawn sandwich; the idea suddenly appealed to Leo too.

He stretched forward across the desk to call out but stopped himself. Claudia was probably already halfway down the stairs and, anyway, prawns had too much cholesterol. He decided to settle for a black coffee and a couple of digestive biscuits.

Leo used to enjoy lunch breaks with Angela when she came to the office, three days a week, to help out. They usually sat together, either side of his desk, with a roast beef and horseradish sandwich each, sometimes cheese and pickle and always with a glass of red wine; just the one. But they hadn't done that for a long time, not for more than a year, maybe even longer. Angela rarely came into the office these days, always too busy at home.

"Do we do topless models?" Sara called from reception, one hand over the mouthpiece of the 'phone. "Bloke wants to know. Something to do with a club."

"Tell him no," Leo grunted. "Our girls are fashion models not floozies."

"Sorry didn't get that," she screamed back. "What did you say?"

"No," said Leo, louder this time. "No topless models."

There was a brief pause before Sara appeared in the doorway. "It's OK, he's hung up. Sounded like a weirdo anyway." She nodded towards the mug by his elbow. "Get you some more coffee?"

"No thanks." He stood up, stretched, rubbed his eyes and pointed to some model cards on a table near the door. "But you could give those to Claudia when she gets back. Book them out for the 'Birds' boutique opening next week. Two hours each, £10 an hour."

Sara flicked quickly through the cards. "Invoice to go to Sambeck is it?."

"Sambeck?" Leo mumbled through a yawn. "What's Sambeck?"

"The company's called Sambeck Ltd," said Sara, looking as

if she'd just sucked on a lemon. "As in Sam and Becky. Naff or what?" She poked out her tongue in disapproval, mouth wide open, picked up the model cards and turned to go. "You tired are you?" she asked as she left the room, without waiting for an answer.

"Bloody tired," he whispered to himself. Leo slumped back wearily into the chair, swung his feet up on to the desk, hands clasped behind his head, and gazed up at the magnificent decorative cornices on the ceiling. He turned slightly, looked across the room to the exquisite carpentry of the panelled wall near the fire place and wondered how long it would survive the new mood for stark simplicity. Tastes were changing, modernisation they called it, but it was little more than vandalism. They ripped out craftsmanship and quality and replaced it with crap like the tasteless, tacky boutiques with idiotic names being stapled together all over London.

He remembered the quaint little ironmonger's shop with the bright green front door, just along from an old-world tobacconist in Carnaby Street. Not so long ago it sold dustbins; today it looked like one, filled with old army uniforms. The ornate brass fittings on the bleached pine walls in the tobacconist shop were long since painted over, purple and black, and now displayed printed T-shirts. Nothing was safe or sacred. One of Leo's favourite pubs in the Kings Road had been ransacked by the Carnaby crowd and degradingly re-opened as a unisex boutique. Even a small church suffered a less than divine transformation into a fashion market selling tat to teenagers with loud, unholy music thudding through stained glass windows into the street.

If boutiques irritated Leo, then the clothes they sold positively incensed him.

Fashion designers, who once knew better, unashamedly stole ideas from movie idols down at the local cinema. Just a few years earlier they'd blatantly copied *Doctor Zhivago* fur trimmed coats and hats for girls, then *Bonnie & Clyde* pin-striped gangster suits for boys, with 'Bonnie' berets for their make-believe molls. Fancy dress, Leo called it. As he told a fashion writer at the time, if *Tarzan* had been big on the film circuit, loin cloths would have been high fashion.

Things had gone from bad to worse since then, much worse. At least a loin cloth provided a small degree of modesty, but as the 'mini' skirt gradually disappeared up its own hemline, girls were now wearing little more than a bandage around their bums.

Leo hauled himself out of the chair and ambled over to the open window, wondering what his favourite fashion designer would have made of the 'micro' skirt. For Leo, at least, Coco Channel's death earlier in the year had somehow formalised the end of elegance. Vulgarity was the name of the new brat on the block and she seemed to have fans everywhere, even down there in up-market Bond Street.

There was no reply when he telephoned Angela again, just before three, and when his four o'clock appointment rang to ask if they could reschedule the meeting for the following week, he decided to call it a day.

"You can get me on the car 'phone for the next hour and at home after that," he announced to anyone who might be listening on his way through reception. The green umbrella was pulled, like Excalibur, from the plant pot and held briefly aloft. He stopped abruptly at the swing doors, turned to remind Sara that he wouldn't be in the following day and waited for a response.

"Best thing," she said nodding her head with great authority. "You look really haggard you do. Tired out."

Leo took a deep breath. "I'll probably be OK if I make it through the night Sara, he sighed. "I'm truly indebted to you for your concern."

Sara watched, expressionless, as the swing doors shuffled to a close.

The black Rolls Royce edged slowly out of Curzon Street, gradually filtered into the traffic jam crawling down Park Lane, then came to a compete standstill at Hyde Park Corner. Leo leaned forward, bared his teeth in the rear view mirror and made a hasty examination of the two front ones before the traffic moved off again. He tapped each in turn with his finger nail and decided there might be a problem with the one on the right. It seemed a bit loose, with irritating twinges, the sort which sometimes developed into something more painful. Probably best to leave well alone, he told himself. Wait and see.

Less than an hour later, with London's traffic far behind and the Surrey countryside stretching out, green and inviting, towards Guildford, he changed his mind. The twinges were now a nagging ache. Leo slowed the car just before Ripley's village post office, turned into the narrow slip road opposite and reversed into a parking space in front of a small parade of shops. A short walk up the road to the dentist then some unpleasant probing, two X-rays, a reassuring smile and he was on his way back in the car with a prescription for antibiotics if they were needed.

Leo paused for a moment in front of the antique shop and peered through the window before going inside to take a closer look at an Art Deco table clock tucked away on a shelf, half hidden behind a portrait of a women, in line with a muddled pile of faded books and a pink-faced china doll. He moved the painting to one side.

"How much?" He nodded casually in the general direction of the clock, blue and white with gold Roman numerals.

An owl-eyed man in a beige cardigan, holes in the sleeves, looked up from behind a desk near the back of the shop. "If you mean the timepiece," he said, "It's £25."

Leo lifted it down from the shelf, quickly looked it over, put it back and turned towards the man at the desk. "The base has been repaired," he said dismissively. "1 could go to £15. No more." He switched his attention briefly to a painting of a windmill, hanging from the handle of a pine cupboard, flicked through the pages of a large leather-bound book then, with a last fleeting glance around the shop, made towards the door.

"I can let you have it for £20. That's my best price." The owl eyes blinked rapidly, waiting for a response.

Leo went slowly back to the shelf, frowned, rubbed his chin and hesitated. "No. I can't go above £15," he said, half-heartedly, trying to control his excitement. There didn't appear to be a signature but he was fairly sure it was made by Cartier; a French classic from the thirties, jade and lapis lazuli design with mother of pearl on the face, possibly worth as much as £1,000.

The clock, ungraciously wrapped in newspaper and wedged into a cardboard box marked 'dog biscuits', was exchanged for three five pound notes then placed carefully on the back seat of the car and driven-off, in style, to its new home. Leo unpacked it in the kitchen, lightly wiped it over with a damp cloth, and placed it in the middle of the pine breakfast table near the window. He stood back to admire his newly-acquired bargain, toothache completely gone.

A dozen long-stemmed red roses, still wrapped in cellophane, were laying on the draining board. The card, inky blue message smeared with coffee dregs, was in the waste bin under the sink, where the remains of breakfast had been splattered over Herb Alpert and his Tijuana Brass. His face hardened as he wiped the cassette, slowly, meticulously with the cloth and placed it on the table beside the clock.

Paddy pushed open the kitchen door with his nose and flopped down in front of the fridge. He was followed cautiously into the room by one of the decorators, crumpled flat cap folded under his arm, wiping his hands with a rag.

"Sorry to trouble you sir," he said, opening the door wider, "but a chap here says he needs to know which fireplace you want taking out." He stepped back and pointed down the hall.

Leo looked mystified for a moment, repeated the word fireplace to himself a few times, then hurried off towards the front door where a man in a navy blue boiler suit at once apologised for being late. Something to do with having to go back to swap trucks with someone else at the yard because he'd taken the wrong load, or it might have been wrong road.

No matter, Leo wasn't in the least bit interested. "What's all this about taking out fireplaces?" he asked curtly.

"Dunno exactly," the man said, taking a slip of paper out of his pocket. "All I've been told is it's an old fashioned one, pre-war they said, and that you want it out." He picked up his bag of tools. "But if someone's got that wrong up at the office I'd best be off." He climbed back into a white builder's truck, bags of cement and a pile of sand neatly stacked in the back and had started off down the drive before Leo could ask any more questions.

A trail of grubby dust sheets, spread haphazardly through the hall and up the stairs, led Leo to the green bedroom where the decorators were now ensconced, with all their paraphernalia, scraping the floral paper from the wall.

He stood, silent, in the doorway, staring at the stain in the middle the floor. Somehow it didn't look quite so bad in daylight and the dank smell of wet wallpaper, soggy strips scattered across the floor, had started to overpower the pungent cocktail of spilled paint and thinners from the night before. "I don't suppose Mrs Gannesh mentioned this business about a fireplace to either of you, did she?" he asked quietly, looking at each of the two men in turn.

They both shook their heads. "Not as such, she didn't. No," said the man with the cap. "But she said not to start on the room downstairs until some building work was finished, what with all the mess it would make." He hesitated for a moment. "I think she must have been waiting-in for someone this morning. Told me she couldn't wait no longer though, just before she went out. Could have been the man about the fireplace I suppose."

Leo managed a tired smile, nodded in agreement and went back to the kitchen. He carefully arranged the roses in a tall pewter vase which he displayed on a square oak table in the hall facing the front door. The Herb Alpert cassette, badly stained but still playable, was returned to the shelf above the eight track then he made himself a cup of coffee, black, no sugar, which he took with him down the hall to the lounge on the 1930's side of the house.

He sat on the edge of the couch, leaning forward, elbows on his knees, admiring the exquisite mirrored Art Deco fire place which, if Angela's morning had gone to plan, would now be on the back of a truck headed for the scrap yard instead of the most important feature of the room. On top, in the centre, the clock took pride of place. It looked even better than he'd imagined; the two were made for each other.

Leo quite surprised himself with his sudden determination to keep the classic style of the thirties extension in tact. Angela's planned mock Tudor make-over was, he decided, completely out of the question and the fireplace was staying exactly where it was. He stood up proudly, lightly stroked the top of the Cartier clock with his finger tips and nodded his silent approval at his new-found resolve.

He'd always left the important decisions about interior decor to Angela. It was her domain, and very good she was at it too, but this time it was different, more important. This time he felt strangely protective, involved, somehow responsible for keeping things the way they were meant to be, the way they were.

Chapter Three

Saturday morning's quiet calm was interrupted at eight o'clock by the clattering din of a lawn mower outside the bedroom window. Angela half opened her eyes, blinked herself into consciousness and raised herself, lazily, on one elbow. She sat up, not yet fully awake, hugging her knees for a few moments, trying to remember if it was duck or pheasant she'd ordered for dinner that evening, before she calling the butcher to ask if he'd be a darling and drop-off whatever it was on his way home.

The top of Leo's head came briefly into view as he reached the end of the garden and turned the noisy, rattling machine around, back towards the house. He'd be at it for hours, getting the stripes on the lawn just right, not crooked and uneven the way the gardeners had left things on Wednesday. This was a good time to ring Tim.

"Good morning. Thatchers."

Angela didn't recognise the eloquent female voice which answered the 'phone, but then Tim changed his staff as often as his underwear. "Is Mr Thatcher available please?" she asked.

"May I say who's calling?"

"Oh just say it's Mrs Jones." She smiled, hummed quietly to herself, their song, the one about the Mrs Jones who had *'a thing going on'*, just like her. The tell-tale clicking on the line, followed by apologies for keeping her waiting, meant the call was being transferred upstairs to Tim's flat. Angela knew he was rarely at his desk before nine.

"Tim Thatcher here. Can I help you?" he said at last.

"Definitely darling," she breathed into the 'phone. "Leo's outside mowing the lawn and I'm here, alone, in bed."

"Then it's about time you got yourself up," he said softly. "You're supposed to be hosting a dinner party this evening."

"I'll make sure you sit you next to me, on my right. We can

41

pretend there's nobody else around."

The lawn mower spluttered to a halt. Quiet. She waited for a moment for it to start up again but, apart from the distant '*cooing*' of a pigeon on the roof, everything was still.

"I'll have to go darling," she whispered. "Leo's either finished the lawn or run out of petrol."

Tim chuckled. "What time do you want us tonight?"

"Seven thirty. And who's 'us'? Who are you bringing?"

"Oh just some gorgeous movie starlet I met at one of Sean Connery's jet-set parties a while back. Long blonde hair, legs up to her bum, you know the type."

Angela gripped the 'phone with both hands. "Be serious you monster. Who's coming with you?"

"Nobody you need worry about, just my new assistant."

"What's she like, how old?" she asked impatiently.

"Frumpy, frigid, fat and well over forty; will that do? Now I really must go. I've got work to do, unlike some people who can lay around in bed all day chatting on the 'phone."

"What's her name?"

"Her names Caroline, Caroline Blanchard. Why?"

Angela didn't answer. She watched, startled, in silence, as Leo, left hand wrapped in a handkerchief, kicked off his shoes in the doorway, hurried across the bedroom into the bathroom and fumbled around for a first aid plaster in the cabinet above the sink.

"What have you done to yourself?" she called after him.

"Nothing serious, just cut my hand on the mower." He poked his head around the door, smiled, waved a blood stained finger then disappeared back into the bathroom. "Who's that on the 'phone?"

"Just the butcher," she said, quickly replacing the receiver. She slipped out of bed, wrapped a lace dressing gown around her shoulders and peered, cautiously, at Leo's hand in the sink. "Is there anything I can do?" she asked, turning away, eyes half closed, teeth clenched, hoping there wasn't.

Leo flinched only slightly as he dripped antiseptic on to his finger from a dark brown bottle. "For starters you could stop looking as if I'd just slit my wrists, then you might get a plaster ready to stick on my finger." He dabbed his hand with a tissue. "It's not life-threatening, just bloody awkward."

Paddy stood up, front paws on the edge of the sink, huffed warm, clammy breath into Leo's face for a moment as Angela pressed down the edges of the plaster then bounced back into the bedroom and off down the stairs well ahead of the urgent ringing at the front door bell.

"Someone's in a flaming hurry," said Leo, quietly preoccupied, checking his front tooth in the mirror, pushing it lightly with his tongue.

Angela shrugged. "I can't go. I'm not dressed yet."

"OK, leave it to me." Leo shuffled slowly across the bedroom, wriggled his feet awkwardly back into his shoes. "Don't you worry yourself, I'll deal with it," he sighed.

Leo's elementary Sulky for *'Why the hell can't you answer the door for a change?'*, was immediately obvious but she chose to ignore it.

"I'm coming, keep your shirt on," he shouted as he made for the front door.

The rhythmic throb of the lorry's engine vibrated across the front of the house as the first of three pallets of bricks was swung outward on a hissing pneumatic arm. "Over there do you will it?" A head appeared through the driver's window, nodding towards the garage block.

"Difficult to get, these," said the driver, pulling hard down on a red lever on the side of the lorry with both hands. "Come from an old house somewhere I wouldn't mind betting."

"Wait just a minute," Leo yelled above the noise from the revving engine, hands waving in front of him, head shaking in disbelief as the pallet thudded to the ground. "There's been some kind of mistake here."

The engine throttled back to a more gentle throb. The delivery docket was quite specific. Reclaimed rustic bricks, it said, ordered and paid for by Mrs A Gannesh.

"No mistake there mate," said the driver. "Your bricks they are, bought and paid for." Two more pallets crunched to the ground alongside the first then he was gone.

"Aren't they beautiful?" Angela's voice, soft, gentle, from the landing window directly above the front door, face cradled in her hands, elbows on the window ledge. "Took me simply ages to find them."

Leo tugged a brick from the first pallet, inspected it, then tossed it back on the pile. "Probably cost the earth too," he snapped. "Anyway, what are they for?" He paused, waiting for a reply, turned and looked up at the window in time to see it slam shut.

Angela was at her dressing table by the time he'd reached the bedroom. She spoke to his reflection in the mirror without turning round. "They're for the new fireplace," she said, brushing her eye lashes with mascara.

"And what new fireplace would that be?" Leo, quietly calm and controlled, stood behind her, hands on hips, legs apart, daring her to make eye contact.

"Oh come on now Leo. Do try to keep up," she chortled, ignoring his gaze and concentrating on her lashes.

"What new fireplace?" he repeated, this time louder, leaning forward over her shoulder.

She looked up, eye contact at last. "The one which is going to replace the mirrored monstrosity in the lounge downstairs. That fireplace," she said firmly.

"Well now isn't that just the strangest thing? I don't remember having that discussion with you, the one when we agreed to rip out an art deco fireplace and replace it with a pile of old bricks."

Her eyes flashed. "There's really nothing to discuss. It's hideous."

"Well I bloody well like it," he yelled.

Angela stood up suddenly, tight lipped, pushed her chair sharply back into his shin and stormed off. "If you're going to lapse into militant Sulky," she screamed from the bathroom, "we'll have to talk about it some other time."

"You can rely on it," said Leo starting towards the door. "And I don't want to find more numskull builders on the doorstep with instructions to remove valuable fireplaces."

She didn't answer. Instead she la la la'd a defiant tune, the way she always did when she didn't want to hear anymore. Not really a tune at all, nothing recognisable, just a disjointed muddle of happy little la la la notes which helped her to block out reality and reason when she was in the wrong.

"Spoilt bloody bitch," he mumbled to himself as he headed back to the relative peace of mowing the lawn.

Angela waved a limp arm royally out of the car window as she neared the gates at the end of the drive ten minutes later. Leo ignored her, crammed another load of grass cuttings on the top of an already groaning wheel barrow and turned away, watching through the corner of his eye as the   Porsche accelerated off in the direction of the village. The distant sound of the church clock said she was late for her three o'clock hairdressing appointment but then Angela was always at least ten minutes late for everything in the bizarre belief that it was the height of bad manners to turn-up on time. She'd long since decided that punctuality created the wrong impression and gave things an unfashionable importance. Arriving at the appointed hour, she'd confided more than once, made you seem far too anxious, much too keen. In Angela's unique etiquette, it was tantamount to taking the last slice of cake.

By the time she returned home, late, at six o'clock Angela was sure that the entire neighbourhood had been told about the business with the Art Deco fireplace. Billowing smoke, rising high above the trees from Leo's bonfire in the vegetable garden, sent smoke signals into an otherwise cloudless sky, messages to the locals in `smoky' Sulky which drifted slowly across the neatly trimmed lawn, out beyond the front of the house and up towards the main road. `Big chief plenty mad with squaw who speak with forked tongue,' they probably said. `Chief go on warpath if happen again - send her to happy hunting ground if squaw not careful.'

Angela smiled at the unlikely picture of Leo in war paint, closed the car window to the pungent fog as she approached the gates then quickly slipped down into second gear and accelerated up towards the house, now basking in the late afternoon sunshine at the end of the drive, a light haze of earlier messages hovering above the rooftop.

Milly, in a crisp yellow cotton dress protected by an apron, white with blue flowers, wiped her eyes with the back of her hand as she peeled the last onion. Four duck breast halves, boned and skinned, to her left on a large round plate and the rest of the ingredients for the Gannesh's favourite Duck a l'Orange, neatly arranged on the table, were quickly inspected without comment as Angela passed through the kitchen on her way upstairs.

"What time do you want to eat?" Milly called after her, wiping chubby fingers with a wet cloth. "Only I've got to be off by nine."

Angela stopped, turned and thought for a moment. "Oh, eightish I suppose. Should give you enough time to do the main dishes before you go. Yes?"

Milly prodded the back of her tightly permed hair with her left hand, chin pressed firmly into the hollow of her neck. She looked down at the floor, refusing to answer.

Angela recognised the indignant look - dangerous ground. "OK then, do as much as you can," she said quietly. "Just do your best."

"I always do my best. Goes without saying." She stalked off towards the fridge, took out some large green olives and chopped them noisily on a board.

At seven thirty on the dot, Giles and Paula Maxwell rang the front door bell, sending Paddy into a sliding, barking frenzy down the stairs and along the hall to greet them.

"Who can that be?" said Angela, unconcerned, checking the hem of her dress in the wardrobe mirror, face on, perfume at peak power, hair loose and shining.

Leo scowled, slipped on his jacket, prepared to leave, then stopped, uncertainly, at the door. "Let's try, at least, to have a civilised evening?" he said solemnly, waiting for a reaction. "Keep it light eh? No nonsense?"

She glared back at him in the mirror, la la la'd spitefully until he'd reached the front door and she could hear voices in the hall.

Paula's gold hoop earrings, heavy, swinging and dangerously large, knocked awkwardly against Leo's nose as he welcomed her with an affectionate kiss on both cheeks. She looked uncomfortable, ill at ease, fiddling self-consciously with a band of tiny round mirrored beads draped, Romany style, across her forehead. Her skirt swished noisily down the hall towards the bar, layers of cascading scarlet and black taffeta topped by a lacy white blouse with puffy sleeves. Giles, one hand protectively on her bottom, steered her across the room over to the stool. She hurriedly lit a cigarette, inhaled deeply and breathed out a long, smoke-filled sigh before she sat down, massaging her forehead with the tips of her fingers.

Something was obviously not quite as it should be but Leo held back from asking any questions until he'd lined-up half a dozen glasses on the top of the bar and carefully filled three of them with Champagne. "Everything OK Paula?" he said, finally, in a matter-of-fact way. "You seem a bit edgy."

Giles stood behind her, lightly rubbed her shoulders. "She's seen something," he said solemnly, without further explanation.

"Seen what?" Leo grinned, moved his head slightly to one side and pushed two glasses of Champagne in the general direction of his guests. "Nothing to do with me I hope," he said, quickly checking his flies.

Paula forced a smile, straightened herself on the stool and sipped her drink. "I saw your face Leo," she said. "It appeared in a strange mist above the house. You were drifting away from us."

A loud gasp. Everyone's attention instantly switched to the female figure silhouetted in the doorway. Angela, motionless, in a black crepe dress, tight, short and plunging, stood silent, serious for just a few seconds then burst into laughter. "Oh Paula darling that was just one of Leo's lingering smoke signals, a self-portrait in the sky. He's really very good at it, aren't you my sweet?" She blew him a kiss as she sauntered over to the bar.

"It wasn't smoke I saw," said Paula emphatically. "It was the mist I always see when I.." she hesitated for a moment before saying the words. "When I see things."

Angela touched her hand reassuringly. "And do you often see things darling? It must be so trying for you."

"Actually it's not trying at all." Paula crumpled the end of her cigarette into a large stone ashtray. "It's a gift," she snapped.

Giles nodded. "That's right. Paula's had it since she was a young child. Psychic vision they call it."

"Well don't you worry yourself about it," Angela quipped. "They can do wonders with corrective lenses these days." She slipped gracefully from the stool, Champagne glass in one hand, smoothing her skirt with the other and headed towards the sound of Paddy's barking, heralding the arrival of a car in the drive.

Paula stared straight ahead, expressionless, head tilted slightly back. Slowly, precisely, she lit another cigarette and turned to Leo. "Does Angela believe in anything," she asked, "anything at all?"

Leo thought for a second. "I think she probably did, once," he said edging out from behind the bar over to the cassette player. "But now she may have lost her nerve."

Giles emptied his glass. "Surely it doesn't take nerve to believe in something does it?"

"Of course it does. When you believe in something you run the risk of being wrong, let down perhaps." Leo slid the eight track cassette into play mode.

The sound of the Tijuana Brass wafted down the hall to greet the new arrivals. Tim, in a white linen suit, beige open-neck shirt, tan suede shoes, cradling a huge bunch of yellow roses, a bottle of Moet and Chandon dangling precariously between finger and thumb, stepped back to introduce his new assistant.

Caroline Blanchard extended a well-manicured hand, smiled broadly and stepped confidently into the hall. "Such a beautiful house," she said quietly, wide brown eyes fixed on her host. "You must be very proud."

Angela stared, unblinking, at the lightly tanned face, high cheek bones, neat chiselled nose and full, generous, mouth. Thick auburn hair, shoulder length and perfectly styled, added a Parisian chic which Angela had so often admired in French models. "We will be when we've finished it," she said, wondering what became of the fat, frigid lady, of forty Tim had described on the `phone. The slim, feminine figure standing in the hall, wearing a particularly un-frumpy Saint Laurent trouser suit, didn't look a day over thirty.

Caroline looked around, excitedly, as Angela led them towards the bar. "What more can you possibly do to such a magnificent house?"

"Quite a lot with any luck," said Angela, now more than mildly irritated by Tijuana trumpets.

Leo had turned down the volume by the time she returned. He looked straight past her to Tim in his white suit. "Four cornets and two choc ices if you please my man," he called across the bar. "Didn't hear the chimes from the van or I'd have come out to meet you."

"I'm surprised you can hear anything above the sound of that squealing record." Angela quickly ejected the cassette. "There now we can all hear ourselves speak," she said, taking hold of Caroline Blanchard's hand. "May I introduce you to our very good friends Paula and Giles Maxwell and, of course, my husband Leo who has no taste whatsoever in either music or interior decor."

Caroline settled herself on a stool, one foot on the floor, unbuttoned her jacket, thrust her thumb into her belt and leaned towards the bar. "Oh, I'm sure that can't be true," she whispered, looking directly at Leo as he handed her the glass of Champagne.

"It isn't true." Paula blew smoke high into the air. "Leo's has excellent taste in most things."

Tim stood back and glanced up at a row of pewter mugs hanging from brass hooks on a narrow shelf above his head. "Surely good taste is all a matter of personal taste, isn't it? We don't all have to like the same things do we?"

Angela laughed and started towards the door. "The punishment for stating the obvious, Mister Thatcher, is to help me put the starters on the table. Do it again and we'll have you washing-up as well." She pushed Tim playfully out of the room.

Giles called after them. "Slip your jacket off Tim, it'll make a fine table cloth."

"Perhaps I could lend a hand," said Caroline. "I don't mind, really."

Leo shook his head. "Wouldn't hear of it." He topped-up each of their glasses. "Tim's quite used to being ordered around in this house. Serves him right for coming round so often."

"Besides," Paula interjected, "he knows by now how Angela likes things done."

A large white tureen of cold vichyssoise soup was placed in the centre of the long oak table, six soup dishes slammed down, noisily, on board table mats with pictures of mediaeval pageantry, before Angela spoke. "Who is she?" she asked, eyes fixed on Tim from the opposite end of the table.

"She's a client actually." Tim polished the silver ladle with a napkin. "Looking for a house this side of Guildford."

"Why did you bring her?"

"Because you told me to bring someone."

"Do you usually take clients out for dinner then?" She grabbed the back of the chair with tightly clenched hands.

"Come on now Angie, she's working for me for a short while, just until she gets settled. Filling-in time really I suppose. I told you on the `phone, she's my new assistant."

"You also told me she looked like a hot air balloon, not Audrey Hepburn."

"Come on now, she works for me, that's all. And besides, I don't fancy skinny birds like Caroline Blanchard."

Angela slowly loosened her grasp of the chair back, smiled weakly. "She is a bit skinny, isn't she?" she said. "Not your type at all."

"I'll call your guests in or the vichyssoise will be cold." He pushed the floppy schoolboy hair out of his eyes and set off to get the others.

Caroline Blanchard, sitting on Leo's right at the far end of the table, ran her finger down the frosty stem of the Lalique wine glass in front of her, exploring the intricate grape design. She stared uneasily at Paula's cigarettes and lighter, placed for easy reach on the side plate opposite and resigned herself to the prospect of a smoky meal ahead.

Paula searched around for an ash tray before she finally sat down, adjusted the gypsy band around her head and finished the glass of Champagne she'd brought with her from the bar.

The intermittent "darling," repeated four or five times from the other end of the table, quietly at first but then louder and with fading affection, had started to sound very much like a reprimand before Leo peered, quizzically, through the candelabra. "Yes," he said as if he'd just answered the door to an unwelcome brush salesman. "What is it?".

Angela, face stretched in a counterfeit smile, nodded towards the decanter. "The wine darling, the wine." She turned away quickly, flicked her shoulder, patted the seat of the chair on her left. "Giles sweetie, sit here next to me," she cooed. "And you Tim, on my right."

"You're obviously a Herb Alpert fan," said Caroline as Leo filled her glass.

Angela winced. "Please don't encourage him Caroline. Leo would play his Herb Alpert cassettes all night given half the chance."

"And why not?" said Leo raising his glass jauntily. "To the best band around."

Caroline smiled. "I'll drink to that."

Tim, elbows on the table, hands clasped, gently nudged his knee into Angela's thigh. Her face slowly softened into a smile, a slight quiver on her lips. She looked away, slipped off her shoe, ran her toe across the back of his leg.

"Fantastic soup Angela." Giles leaned back in the chair and dabbed his mouth with his napkin, looking expectantly towards the tureen.

"There's plenty more if you'd like some," she said. "Please help yourself."

She glanced around the table. Paula, wearing her silly occult expression, examining Leo's injured finger, tracing the lines in his palm, predicting the painfully obvious. Caroline listening, nodding politely, stroking the side of her face with long, slender fingers, slightly bored. Leo, aware, trying to retrieve his left hand, perhaps change the subject, and Giles, dear Giles, oblivious, hunched over a second bowl of vichyssoise. Tim's hand touched hers under the table and nobody knew. Just a fleeting squeeze but totally secret. It made her feel alive, dangerous, romantic and wonderfully juvenile. She was suddenly aware of Caroline's gaze which softened into a gentle smile before, finally, she spoke.

"You really must put a stop to this right now Angela?" she said softly. "Paula says Leo's going on a long journey - alone."

Angela laughed, took hold of her glass with both hands. "Oh, that'll probably be his boring two-day business trip to Manchester next week. And Paula's quite right, of course, I won't be going. Can't stand the place."

"It wasn't 'Manchester I saw," said Paula abruptly. "And it wasn't business either."

"Sounds like one of Leo's dirty weekends in Brighton to me." Giles prodded Caroline's arm with his elbow, winked. "Sly old dog, he is."

Tim tapped the side of his glass with a spoon bringing the table to order. "I have a question for you all," he announced. "Why, pray, is Brighton the preferred location for a dirty weekend?"

"Easy," said Giles. "It's the perfect alibi, a good excuse. You tell people you are going to Brighton for the sea air when, in fact, you never ever see the sea."

"Then why not Hastings or Southend?" Tim folded his arms, not really expecting an answer. "I'll tell you what I think," he said after a few moments. "It's all about being discreet, not being found out."

Angela didn't like the new direction of the conversation, not one bit. She quickly reached across for Tim's soup dish, slipped a wayward foot back into her shoe and made a vengeful stab at his ankle as she stood up.

He looked at her in surprise. "Can I give you a hand?" he said rising unsteadily to his feet.

"No thank you Tim, sit yourself down. You've done quite enough already this evening." She collected up the rest of the soup dishes and left the room.

Paula re-lit a half smoked cigarette, brushed up some bread crumbs with a serviette and placed them in the ash tray. She leaned forward, took a deep breath and wagged a small spoon at Caroline on the other side of the table. "I'm not picking you up," she said, her eyes narrowing. "I usually see an aura."

Caroline smiled. "I'm not sure I've got one."

"Everyone's got one, some better than others, but they've always got one. Like a coloured light."

"What could have happened to mine then? It all sounds quite worrying."

"Perhaps it's being suppressed in some way; covered up." Paula tapped the back of her hand with the spoon and stared around the room. "Maybe there are too many other vibrations in here. I'm not sure."

Caroline tried her best to look suitably impressed. "Goodness," she gasped, "how absolutely fascinating Paula. You seem to know such a lot about these things."

"It's a gift," said Giles solemnly. "Psychic vision. She was born with it."

Leo flinched then turned to Caroline, the hint of a grin on his face. "As Paula seems to be having a bit of a psychic block with your aura perhaps you should tell us all a bit about yourself."

"There's really not a lot to tell." She sat motionless in the chair, looking down at the wine glass, hands in her lap. "Honestly, I'm extremely uninteresting."

She reminded Leo of a small child who'd just been asked to recite a poem to amuse the adults. It made him feel suddenly clumsy, tactless, and slightly guilty; annoyed that he hadn't considered the possibility that Caroline Blanchard might not want to talk about herself.

He placed a comforting hand on her arm. "Do forgive me," he said. "I didn't mean to give you the third degree."

Caroline looked up slowly and smiled. "Don't be silly Leo, nothing to forgive. I just don't want to bore you all to tears."

Tim, right arm draped casually over the back of the chair, twisted himself round towards her and slowly sipped his wine. He stared at her for a moment before he spoke. "Such false modesty doesn't become you Caroline. Shame on you."

The Duck a l'Orange, held high on a willow patterned dish, was ceremoniously delivered to the centre of the table by Milly, tea towel over one arm, scowl on her face, followed by Angela, carrying the plates.

"Well done," said Giles draping his serviette over his tie, banging the table with his hand. "That looks good enough to eat."

"Too greasy for my stomach, duck is." Milly wiped her hands on the tea towel. "Even the smell of it's enough to turn me over." She span around quickly and headed back to the kitchen to collect the couscous.

"I'm afraid Milly's a gourmet hypochondriac," said Leo. "A wonderful cook who hates food. Says everything makes her ill."

Milly returned with the couscous and placed it down in front of Angela. She stood back for a moment looking round the table as if she'd forgotten something, wiped her hands, for a second time with the tea towel. "I'd have two veg with it myself. But if you like Arab food, steamed semolina, well….." She left without finishing the sentence, shutting the door behind her.

Paula flicked the ash from her cigarette and waited for the duck to be served-up on plates, everyone ready to eat, before she finally and reluctantly squashed it into the ash tray. A short pause between the duck and the baked Alaska and again after the stilton emptied her cigarette case for the evening. She snapped it shut for good at about half past ten, visibly irritated and grumbling at Giles for not reminding her to bring a spare pack of her favourite Styvesant.

They abandoned the dining room, still hazy with cigarette smoke, for coffee in the lounge, a happily tobacco-free zone where the scent of the summer evening drifted in from the garden through the open doors. Three wide sofas, deep buttoned in rich chestnut leather, formed a comfortable square with the inglenook fireplace, piled high with logs - a rustic backdrop for a porcelain vase filled with huge yellow sunflowers.

Caroline sipped her coffee, sank back into the sofa and gazed up at the oak beam which spanned the inglenook. "It's just beautiful. So very simple, basic and completely wonderful." She turned to Tim, standing by the window, hands in pockets, looking out over the pool. "Could you find me a house with a fireplace like this one?"

"No need to," said Angela. "You can make your own from reclaimed materials. We're going to build one similar to this in the other lounge. You probably saw the bricks in the drive."

Leo, bent uncomfortably over a low wooden side table, pressed hard down on the small round knob on top of the coffee plunger, and watched it sink gradually to the bottom of the glass percolator. He straightened up, slowly, eyes fixed on Angela, rubbing a small red mark on the palm of his hand. "Actually Angela's got that slightly wrong. In fact we're not going to build another fireplace in the other lounge at all."

Angela flopped down onto the sofa next to Caroline, lightly flicked her hair with the tips of her fingers and spoke into space. "Oh I see. We'll just keep that art deco monstrosity instead, shall we?"

"Exactly darling." Leo poured two cups of coffee, handed them to Giles and Paula. "We'll keep it just as it is if you don't mind."

"Right." The terse reply, more challenge than agreement, brought silence to the room.

Caroline was the first to speak. "It's always difficult to know what to do for the best," she said cheerfully. "I'm sure you'll make the right decision."

Tim moved away from the French doors across the room to Leo, offered his empty cup for a refill. "Why don't you show Caroline the other fireplace Leo? She seems to know quite a lot about thirties design and architecture."

"Would you?" Caroline straightened up. "I'd love to see it."

"You can have it with my blessing." Angela crossed her legs and folded her arms in one swift movement. "It looks like something you might win at a fair ground, all glitzy and garish."

Leo smiled. "What Angela is trying to tell you is that it's mirrored. But come and see for yourself."

The dog led the way, bounded down the hall then pushed past them both into the room as soon as Leo opened the door. Caroline stood for a short while framed in the doorway, staring across at the fireplace and Leo's new clock. "Perfect," she said eventually. "César and Cartier together."

"Do you really think it is?" Leo picked up the bargain timepiece, excited, turned it over. "There's no signature but I thought it was a Cartier the moment I saw it."

Caroline knelt down in front of the magnificent angular surround, her face reflected in the tiny pieces of mirrored mosaic. "I'm fairly sure about the clock but absolutely certain about the fireplace." She reached out and gently touched it as if it might not be real and could disappear in a moment like a bubble. "César," she whispered to herself almost reverently. Then to Leo; "He was a sculptor."

Leo felt slightly uncomfortable, an intruder at a very private reunion of two old, dear friends. He returned the clock to its place of honour and watched, unspeaking, as Caroline sat back on her heels, relaxed, staring into the empty fireplace. She slowly raised her head, a look of supreme contentment on her face, smiling back at him through the jagged mirror patchwork. "Hello you," she said softly.

He heard himself answer, something, perhaps it was just `hello', he wasn't sure. Not important. The words really didn't matter.

Paddy lolloped across the room, tail wagging, licked the side of her face enthusiastically and left again as quickly as he'd arrived.

"What's the verdict?" Tim leaned, one hand on the door knob, arm straight. "Is it the real thing?"

"Definitely," said Caroline, rising to her feet. "No doubt about it whatsoever." She took hold of Leo's arm, steadied herself, then quickly smoothed her trousers with her hand.

Leo cleared his throat self-consciously, clapped his hands just once, decisively and made towards the door. "Perhaps we should join the others," he said. "Must be wondering what's happened to us."

"Actually I came to tell you the Maxwells were leaving." Tim yawned. "I think Paula's having nicotine withdrawal symptoms."

Giles dawdled in the hall, happy to linger while Paula collected her things together. "It's been a wonderful evening," she said, kissing Angela on both cheeks. She turned to Leo at the front door. "And you look after yourself. Don't work so hard, it's not worth it."

Tim called out after her. "I'll bring Caroline over for a sharpener after work one evening next week, introduce her to some of the `Kings Oak' locals, so polish up the brass."

"I'm sure Caroline would absolutely hate it," said Angela in a brittle voice.

Caroline reached out for Angela's hand and gave her a gentle hug. "You're quite right. I'm not really a pub person but they tell me the restaurant is really very good." She buttoned her jacket, tugged at the sleeves. "I hope you'll let me repay your kind hospitality; have dinner with me, the two of you, one evening soon? Tim too if he's free."

"We'd love to," said Leo.

Tim shrugged and juggled his car keys. "Fine with me." He started towards the car. "You fix a date, I'll fit in."

Angela looked past them out across the drive as Tim settled himself in the car, picked up the single red rose she placed on the dashboard and read her scribbled note. He looked up, winked, and placed them carefully in the glove compartment.

She smiled, leaning back against the porch, arms folded and blew a secret kiss.

Caroline waved a white silk handkerchief through the open window of the car until it reached the end of the drive and roared off into the night.

Then silence.

Chapter Four

Two dusty days in Manchester weren't really enough to assess the potential for a northern office but by late afternoon on the Wednesday, when his cold seemed to be at it's peak, Leo made an executive decision. He'd drop the idea and go home to bed.

A summer cold, the chemist called it when he picked up the tablets, throat lozenges and three boxes of tissues for the drive back to Surrey. Possibly the raw, tender nostrils reflected in the rear view mirror did have a more summery glow than with a winter cold, the streaming eyes a slightly redder, rosier tinge - hard to tell. And then the rain. Summer rain they said, but rain just the same, loud, determined rain which machine gunned the car's windscreen all the way to the M1 where the sun eventually forced its way through the clouds and declared a temporary cease-fire.

Leo and the weather brightened up nearer to home. Some people, he supposed, might say he was foolish not to stick to the model agency business which he knew so well but after a dismal forty eight hours in Manchester, property investment in Surrey suddenly seemed very appealing. The plan was uncomplicated; he'd buy a few houses, nothing too expensive, tart them up, then rent them out, fully furnished, to visiting Americans or anyone else for that matter.

Three days later, one spent in bed, nostrils almost back to normal, Leo parked his car, paid the five pee for a two hour stay and set off down the high street towards Thatchers estate agents. He stopped off at the bookshop, browsed around for nothing in particular and left, soon after, both hands pressed into the jacket pockets of a grey flannel suit, a book about Surrey wedged under his arm. Then along to the newsagent for a copy of `Country Life'. He stood in the doorway, apprehensive, staring across the road at the dark green shop front, quaint little bow windows either side of the door. Not the ideal windows for an estate agents, no room to display things, but attractive all the same.

Two young girls, gangly legs on wobbly shoes, giggled together at the bus stop, self-consciously pushing and prodding each other. An impromptu performance for a couple of youths on motor bikes who `vroom', 'vroom'ed a deafening response, legs astride, feet firmly on the ground. Three buses happily ignored while the ritual progressed. Tight, white T-shirts, quickly adjusted for maximum exposure. Gloved hands beckoning at last, the bumptious tilt of goggled heads, revving engines and away; two squealing passengers, gripping black leather jackets, off in the direction of the river.

Leo watched them disappear into the traffic, ritual completed, no words spoken. He looked back anxiously across the road to Thatchers, remembering the eight year old schoolboy who'd waited opposite Beryl Thomson's house, not really sure if she was at home or out somewhere but happy to be there all the same, where Beryl *might* be. And now, a life-time later, the feeling was exactly the same.

A small brass bell bounced about on a coiled spring above the door, jangling his arrival to two unoccupied mahogany desks either side of the room and a bank of filing cabinets near the back, drawers labelled from A to Z. Rose pink carpets and cream walls, covered almost entirely with pictures of houses. Leo sat down on a padded bench seat by the window and waited.

More jangling bells then Caroline Blanchard in the doorway. "So sorry," she said, walking straight over to her desk. "Nipped out for some stamps." She put the stamps in a small tin box, clicked it shut and turned around. "Oh my goodness," she screamed, arms outstretched. "It's you."

Leo stood up awkwardly, dropped the book and magazine on the seat behind him, and took her hands. "You'd better not get too near," he sniffed. "I've had a terrible cold."

"I don't catch colds." She smiled, gave him a gentle, hug and stepped back to look at him. "Anyway, what are you doing here? Not moving from that beautiful house surely?"

"Thinking about buying a couple of properties to rent out." Leo, hands behind his back, glanced hurriedly at some of the photographs on the wall. "Not sure what, haven't decided exactly where, not even too clear on how much." He turned to face her. "Actually I'm not really sure about anything. The truth is I think I'm probably here to see you,"

"Good," she said jauntily, apparently unsurprised by Leo's quiet confession. "I hoped that's why you were here."

"You don't mind then?"

She shook her head and sat down at the desk. "What's to mind?"

"Being chatted-up by a silly old bugger like me who should know better."

Her eyes grew wider with her smile. "But you're not," she said, busying herself with some papers on the desk. "And besides, as far as I'm aware I haven't been chatted-up yet so you'd better get on with it."

Leo wasn't sure how long Tim Thatcher had been standing in the archway which led to the back office, staring down, motionless, at a strip of white paper in a plastic bag.

"I was two flaming minutes," he grunted. "They must be hiding in shop doorways just waiting to pounce." He threw the parking ticket in the waste bin then turned to shake hands. "Sorry Leo, rude of me. How are you?".

"Lousy," said Leo. "I was just telling Caroline, I've been laid low with a cold for a few days. First day out."

Tim pulled out the N to P drawer of one of the cabinets and flicked through some files. "So is this a social or business call?

"Strictly business. I'm after a couple of houses to rent out."

"Then you've come to the right place, hasn't he Caroline."

Tim turned to her, grinned, took a file from the cabinet and started towards the back door of the office. "Back in an hour or so," he called out. "Have fun children." The door clunked closed behind him.

They heard the car pull away along the service road then watched it come around to the front of the shop and head off down the high street. Tim hooted as he passed.

"I'm afraid the bugger heard us," Leo mumbled, peering out through the bow window.

"Nonsense." Caroline relaxed back in the chair. "There was nothing to hear."

Leo nodded, hoping she might be right. But what did it matter anyway? Tim could think whatever he liked. To hell with him.

"This is all a bit bloody ridiculous Caroline," he said, flopping back down on the window seat. "I've only just met you, I know absolutely nothing about you and yet here I am scared to death you'll disappear out of my life as quickly as you arrived." He rubbed the palms of his hands together nervously and looked up at her. "That doesn't make any damned sense either, does it? I mean you're not even in my life yet and never likely to be, not in the way I'd like anyway. Look at you, young, attractive, your whole life ahead of you and me in my dotage, on my last legs. What the hell am I talking about?"

"You're talking about the way we look," she whispered. "I'd prefer to talk about who we are, you and I. Us, the two people inside."

"Surely it's much the same thing?"

She wrinkled her nose and winked. "For the moment," she said. "But only for the moment."

Leo wondered why he hadn't noticed the freckles before, just a few across the bridge of her nose. And the deep brown eyes, somehow darker than before, almost black. He rested his chin on two clenched fists, elbows on knees. "So who are you

Miss Blanchard?" he said quietly. "Where did you come from, why are you here?"

"Not much to tell," she said leaned forward across the desk. "I was born and grew up in this part of the world, went away for a while and now here I am back again. I told you on Saturday, I'm really very boring."

Leo sighed. "Boring or not, I want to know all about you." He stood up, buttoned his jacket and prepared to leave. "Perhaps you could play truant one afternoon? Maybe we could go somewhere, have a bite of lunch."

"I'd love to," she said. "When?"

"Well, let's see. No need to rush things." Leo took a black leather diary from his inside pocket, flicked through to June and ran his finger down the page. "Today's the sixteenth," he rubbed his chin thoughtfully, snapped the diary closed and slipped it back into his pocket. "What about today then? Right now in fact."

Caroline glanced across the road to the large square clock above the chemist. It was five past twelve. "Right now would be just perfect," she said, gathering up a pair of white gloves and the small leather handbag which complimented her pale blue dress.

The scribbled note left on Tim Thatcher's desk said she'd be out for the rest of the afternoon, showing Leo around half a dozen rental properties. She didn't think she'd be back and would see him in the morning. A *'Closed-for-Lunch'* sign tapped against the glass panels of the front door as it clicked shut and she turned the key in the lock. They stood together for a moment in the warm sunshine before walking slowly down the high street towards the car park.

Three types of supermarket cheese, one particularly French and smelly, a `special offer' Beaujolais which came complete with two plastic wine beakers taped to the sides of the bottle, carefully arranged in a large brown paper carrier bag with a selection of freshly-baked rolls, different shapes and sizes, from the next door bakery. And all packed neatly away in the boot of the car before they set off for Dorking and an alfresco lunch.

Shafts of bright sunlight flickered through the filigree tunnel of trees, arched gracefully across Abinger's narrow country lanes, gnarled roots bulging through the steep mossy banks on either side, a web of precarious crevices for clinging flowers. Then out from the leafy shadows to a patchwork of open fields, in the distance the muffled hum of a tractor, green baize hills sloping sharply away, speckled with sheep and above it all, edge to edge, the bluest of skies, one solid colour, cloudless.

Caroline stared out through the open car window, her auburn hair gently blowing in the warm breeze, slim brown sunglasses on top like a tiara. "Days like this make me feel terribly vulnerable." She whispered, nestling closer to Leo. "As if I might just be dreaming and will wake up in a moment to find it all gone."

Leo sounded his horn, three loud blasts which shattered the quiet calm of the countryside. "If you heard that," he said, eyes fixed on the twists and turns of the narrow road ahead, "you're definitely not dreaming. Today is guaranteed to stay completely real, at least until nightfall."

She grasped his hand. "You haven't yet told me where we're going?"

"To the top of Surrey," he announced proudly. "To the very tip, the highest point in the whole of the south east."

The view from Leith Hill was everything Leo had promised; a sky high landscape of dazzling shades of green which rolled away from the heavens down to the lower world from which they'd travelled, then gradually faded into misty purple where the distant hills touched the horizon. They left the delights of an eighteenth century Gothic tower to the chattering groups of mortals who queued, patiently, to climb its spiralling steps upwards towards the gods and made, instead, for the cool of a lower wooded area hidden beyond a sea of Rhododendrons, a sensible distance from the crowded peak of the hill which, it was said, offered a vista of seventeen counties to visitors with sufficiently good eyesight.

Beaujolais, bread and Brie, spread on a tartan car blanket in the shade of a craggy oak, a leisurely meal as near to heaven as anyone gets on a June afternoon. Leo laying back, eyes closed, hands clasped behind his head, tie consigned to a jacket pocket and Caroline sitting, shoes off, feet tucked under, completely relaxed.

"Are you in love with me?" she asked, brushing his chin with a buttercup.

He didn't answer.

"It's OK," she said, "the buttercup knows." She gently plucked the yellow petals and placed them ceremoniously, one by one, on Leo's lips.

"He loves me, he loves me not, he loves me: ...."

Her voice gradually faded into a whisper.

Leo opened his eyes and puffed away the petals. "What's the answer? Is it good news or bad?"

"Bright, bright as fallen flakes of light.   Was it L.M Montgomery who wrote that?" she said quietly. "No matter, our special buttercup said you love me."

Leo sat up, resting on his elbow. "Word travels fast in the flower kingdom. I only found out myself this morning."

"You're just a bit slow catching on." She moved closer and touched his lips with her finger. "I don't suppose you've even worked out yet that the feeling's mutual."

"Should we check with the buttercups?"

"Don't be silly. They all know, have done for ages."

Caroline stared up at a small red kite which bobbed above the trees near the crown of the hill. It swayed from side to side like a playful pup trying to escape its leash, then soared higher, taut fabric vibrating in the breeze, finally hovering in one spot above the other earthbound onlookers.

"Everyone should have some time to float up beyond the crowds like that," she said wistfully. "When it was your turn, the special person you're meant to meet in life would look up and know exactly where to find you."

Leo turned over, head back, shielding his eyes from the bright sunlight with his hand, looking up at the kite.

"Do you seriously believe that everyone has a special person in life, someone they're meant to meet?" He turned back to look at her.

"Definitely," she said emphatically. "That's exactly the way it's meant to be."

He poured the last of the wine, handed her a half-filled plastic beaker. "Then why isn't the world filled with blissfully happy couples?"

"Because they are not always fortunate enough to find each other."

"Seems to me they very rarely, if ever, find each other if the divorce rate's anything to go by."

Caroline sighed. "It's quite possible to meet your special person and yet fail to recognise them," she said. "And that's so very sad."

"So what happens then?"

"The worst thing imaginable." Her voice was hushed, a fleeting sadness in her eyes. "You miss each other for a whole lifetime, that's what happens." She put the wine to her lips then quickly placed it to one side on the grass and stood up, self-consciously brushing the front of her dress with her hand.

Leo stared at her for a moment. "Is there something wrong?" he asked. "Something I've said?"

She looked away, searching the sky for the small red kite. It had gone; in its place a brightly coloured paper butterfly dipped and dived across the tree tops at the command of the unseen kite flyer somewhere on the ground below.

"I'm fine, really I am," she said. "But perhaps we should be going. It's quite late, nearly six."

Leo stood up, took hold of her hands and gently squeezed. "When will I see you again?"

Her face softened. "Whenever you want to."

"Like Romeo and Juliet perhaps. Forbidden lovers with secret assignations but with the added complication that, like Romeo's dad, I've got a wife back at home."

The red kite appeared briefly above the tower as they walked slowly back to the car. A small boy, short grey trousers, school socks crumpled around his ankles, arms outstretched, eyes half closed against the sun, gazed up at the fluttering silhouette as it climbed higher into the evening sky, then pulled away across the brow of the hill down towards the car park.

They sat quietly together in the car for a while, looking out beyond the trees over the sun drenched landscape before Leo slipped the key into the ignition and started the car. He turned it off again almost immediately.

"Seriously Caroline," he whispered, "when can I see you again?"

"As I said before, you can see me whenever you want to. Tonight if you like. On the stroke of midnight."

"Midnight?" Leo sank back into the seat. "I can't just creep out of the house in the dead of night like some lovelorn vampire."

"I wouldn't expect you to creep anywhere. Besides, what ever would Angela think if she saw you?"

"I don't suppose she'd even notice, but that's not really the point."

"The point," said Caroline twisting herself around to face him, "is that you don't have to *go* anywhere to reach me."

Leo stared at her in silence, a look of anticipation on his face, waiting for her to continue.

She hesitated for a moment, smoothed out the fingers of her gloves and set them neatly on her lap. "We'll meet in the Red Square," she said without looking up. "It's very simple but you have to concentrate."

He slowly nodded his head. "I'm probably a bit slow on the uptake but where, exactly, is this Red Square?"

"Well, it's not exactly anywhere. It's sort of in our minds."

"Aha," said Leo, as if everything was suddenly crystal clear. "I've seen Paula Maxwell do this one in the pub. Someone thinks of a place, concentrates hard on the name and you have to tell them where it is. Right?"

"Wrong." Caroline slapped his arm with the gloves. "It's not a party trick."

"In that case it'll be far too complicated for me to understand."

"Rest your head back and close your eyes," she said placing a cool hand on his forehead. "Now, what do you see?"

"I can't see anything."

"Surely there's a colour?"

"Not really. It's all just dark purple, almost black."

"Fine, that's a colour. Now try to picture a small red dot right in the centre."

Leo sat quietly for a few seconds then opened his eyes, blinked rapidly and straightened himself up. "There's only dark purple," he said impatiently. "No red dots."

Caroline gently moved his head towards her and looked into his eyes. "You're just not concentrating, are you?" she sighed. "With a bit more patience and a little practice you'll definitely see a tiny red dot right in front of you, I promise. Usually it starts off very small but then gradually grows into a square which fills the whole picture in your mind."

"OK, let's say I see this big red square eventually. What then?"

"Then you think of the special someone in your life and try

to picture them in the square. After a while you'll see them, clearly, as if they were right there with you."

Leo fidgeted about, arms folded, the look of a petulant child creeping across his face. "But they won't be right there with you, will they?"

"Not physically, no," she said quietly. "But when two people see each other in the red square at exactly the same time, it's the next best thing." She waited for his reaction.

"Not quite the same as making love then?" he said staring blankly at the dashboard. "Nothing like it in fact. So it's back to my original question, when can I see you again?" He started the engine and they moved off slowly out from the car park and back down the hill.

"Tomorrow. We'll go and look at some houses for your rental investment - only this time for real?"

"Good idea," he said. "Very good idea indeed."

Leo turned on the radio, twiddled the tuning knob speedily through a noisy hotchpotch of pirate station `pop' and eventually found the end of the BBC's six o'clock news.

"I hope you don't mind. Just wanted to check what's been going on in the world while we've been away."

Caroline, eyes half closed, slowly shook her head. "Don't mind me," she murmured. "I hope you'll forgive me but I'm not really interested in the rest of the world."

Local authorities had been protesting at Education Secretary Mrs Thatcher's plans to end free school milk while they had been sipping Beaujolais on Leith Hill. Elsewhere Mrs Ghandi had sealed the border with Bangla Desh to keep out the refugees and the Government had announced plans to build 1,000 miles of motorways by the 1980's. Leo groaned at the late news of EEC negotiator Geoffrey Rippon's deal to join the Common Market.

"Bloody disaster," he repeated three or four times. "Hundreds of millions of pounds a year to join a club whose members are some of our worst enemies."

Caroline smiled drowsily, eyelids fluttering as the mottled sunlight filtered through the trees to her face. "It seems so unfair," she said. "That awful war, so much unhappiness for such a long time and now its all to be forgiven and forgotten, as if it never happened." She turned towards him and slowly opened her eyes. "Why did it happen Leo? Was there a point to it?"

"It's all about power," he said. "Germany started the war for control of Europe. That didn't work so now they've started a club to do the same thing. Nothing's changed, only the tactics."

"I wish we could have joined a club instead of a war in 1939." She turned off the radio and sidled across the seat towards him, snuggling into his arms, resting her head on his shoulder. "I don't want to hear anymore. Is that OK?"

Leo kissed her hair. "Perfectly OK," he said quietly.

The evening traffic dawdled through the narrow lanes and it was nearly seven by the time they reached Guildford. Leo stopped the car in a quiet side street.

"I've just realised," he said. "I've no idea where you live, where to drop you."

"Drop me at Thatchers, would you?" she said, checking her make-up in the sun visor mirror. "I've got a few things to catch-up on." She quickly put on her gloves and slipped her sunglasses into her handbag. "In fact you could drop me here if you like. It's just a short walk down the High Street and you won't have to turn the car around."

"If that's what you want.   But it's no trouble."

"No really. This will do fine." She opened the car door. "What time will you come by tomorrow?"

"What time would you like me?"

"Say ten thirty. I'll arrange for your first viewing at eleven o'clock. Is that OK?"

"Fine." Leo hesitated for a moment. "Perhaps we could try

your Red Square tonight."

She stepped out of the car and turned back to face him. "Where will you be at midnight?"

"In bed."

"Perfect. Then so will I," she said. "Try your hardest. It's really quite easy if you practice."

Leo watched her walk slowly away from the car, cross the road and turn the corner into the busy High Street without looking back. She reappeared almost at once, just as he'd hoped she would, blowing kisses with both hands and waving frantically before finally heading off down the High Street towards Thatchers.

He felt instantly alone, already missing her, only mildly comforted by the faint scent of her perfume which still lingered in the car, realising at once that he'd never felt this way about anyone before. The short journey back to 'Pelham Green Farm House' passed unnoticed like a dream, soon to be shattered by a series of rapid blasts from a car horn somewhere behind him.

The powder blue Porsche passed him near the entrance to the drive, music blaring, shingle flying, then raced up towards the house where it screeched to a dusty halt in front of the garage block. Two large green Harrods bags burst out from the front seat slightly ahead of the blue denim jeans and black leather zipper jacket topped by a baseball cap.

"Be a love and get the other two bags from the back seat would you?" Angela made for the front door, kicked it open with the heel of her boot and went quickly inside.

Leo rubbed his eyes, sat back and stared at the garage doors, disorientated and confused. Everything had changed, without warning, in one short, wonderful afternoon. Now, in an instant, he was with the wrong person, in the wrong place; an impostor, somehow detached from reality, a player in a meaningless charade. He looked at himself in the rear view mirror and wondered if Angela would notice the difference. It didn't really matter, none of it mattered anymore. Like a recently completed jigsaw puzzle, neatly displayed on a table, his world had been tossed in the air and was now scattered haphazardly across the floor, interlocking pieces in a picture from yesterday which could never be reassembled.

Paddy's boisterous greeting, paws on shoulders, briefly pinning him against the car door, helped to nudged the world back into focus. Then Angela's face at the kitchen window. "Phone call, for you," she yelled.

He collected the two Harrods bags from her car, placed them with the others at the bottom of the stairs and walked slowly into the kitchen. "Who is it?" he asked.

Angela waggled the telephone receiver in front of him impatiently, arm outstretched. "Caroline Blanchard," she said abruptly. "Says she's got dozens of houses for you to see tomorrow, something like that." She dropped the 'phone into the fruit bowl and quickly left the room.

He waited for the tell tale creak of the stairs at the half landing, hand over the mouth piece, before he spoke. "Is everything OK?" he whispered. "Where are you?"

"I'm in the office sorting out your schedule for tomorrow, and I'm fine." She paused for a moment. "Can you speak?"

"Yes, no problem. Angela's upstairs."

"Well I was just thinking. You might find it more straightforward if we meet in the moon tonight instead of the Red Square."

"Bugger". Leo sat down at the kitchen table, tut-tutted a few times. "The moon eh?" he sighed. "Wouldn't you just bloody know it." More sighs, this time louder, more tutting.

Caroline broke in. "What ever's the matter?"

"Just a bit disappointed, that's all," he said wearily. "At long last I have an opportunity to wear my Dan Dare silver foil space outfit and it's away at the cleaners."

He chuckled to himself, reached for a grape, waited for the

response. She didn't answer.

"Hello. Are you still there?"

The line went dead.

Leo looked across to the cork notice board near the fridge, quickly checked the long list of telephone numbers, and called Thatchers. The number rang out no more than three or four times before he carefully redialled, checking each digit in turn, and waited. No reply. His finger traced down the list to `Tim's Flat' underlined in red in the bottom right hand corner. Tim answered almost at once.

"Hi Tim. It's Leo." He cleared his throat. "Sorry to bother you. Nothing important. Er, just wondered if you could let me have Caroline Blanchard's number. I need to check the arrangements for tomorrow."

"She hasn't got one, not yet anyway," said Tim. "I think she said it's being installed next week: Anything I can do?"

Leo hesitated. "No, really. It's not important. I'll call her in the morning."

A wave of panic gripped him as he slowly replaced the receiver and flopped back into the chair, all too aware that he had no way of contacting Caroline Blanchard until the next morning. But what if she wasn't there? Suppose she didn't turn up to work; not tomorrow, not any day? She might just leave Thatchers altogether. Possibly she could be taken ill or maybe have an accident? He cursed himself for the stupid Dan Dare joke which had obviously upset her.

The clickety clack of stiletto heels in the hall, then a waft of perfume as the door opened and Angela, wearing a wispy little red dress which left little to the imagination, twirled into the room. She arranged herself in front of the kitchen window, the light behind her for maximum visual impact, hands clasped into her waist, accentuating the flimsy top. "What do you think?" she purred.

Leo stared at the delicate fabric and decided there was not

much more to it than a spider's web. "I can see your boobs," he said eventually with a frown. "Shouldn't you be wearing a bra?"

"Don't be such a prude." She fluffed up the skirt, twirled around again. "Isn't it beautiful?"

He stood up and poured himself a glass of water, then turned to her, leaning casually against the sink. "I'd call it blatant and cheap," he snapped.

"Blatant if you like darling," she said. "But it certainly wasn't cheap." She opened the fridge door. "What do you fancy for dinner?"

"Can't say I'm very hungry."

"Why don't we just have a quick bite at The Kings Oak' then? I could Christen my dress."

Leo smiled weakly. "You could show off your boobs you mean, don't you?"

"If you've got it, flaunt it." She swished her long hair from side to side with the arrogant flick of her head he knew so well. Then with a theatrical flutter of her eye lids, she stepped slowly, gracefully away from the fridge and sat down at the kitchen table, arms neatly folded in front of her. "Something wrong with my boobs?" she asked quietly.

"They're bloody exhibitionists - the pair of them."

"You've never complained before." She straightened herself up and raised her head. "Do you still fancy me?"

"Every man you've ever met fancies you." He looked away towards the garden. "But you don't need me to tell you that."

"Isn't that what you wanted - a wife they all *fancy,* a pretty appendage to the husband they all *envy?"*

He nodded slowly, turned back to face her. "It's true," he said. "That's exactly what I wanted."

"And now?"

"And now?" he said, starting towards the door. "Now I'm going to take the dog for a walk."

Leo took the lead from the hook above the cupboard, clapped his hands for the dog and strode off into the garden, Paddy close on his heels.

Angela called after him. "I'll take that as a *no* then shall I?"

He turned, looked back at her, forced a fragile smile. "Whatever," he shouted. "I won't be long."

Paddy had barely squeezed himself through the half open side gate and into the field when the Porsche came noisily into view between the trees on the upper road, heading for the dual carriageway. Leo watched it disappear at the cross roads before following Paddy down towards the copse on the far side of the field.

He guessed Angela would be off to Helen's. She never needed much of an excuse to visit her mother. It wasn't Thursday but this would be an interim, unscheduled, emergency visit. They'd probably sit together in the small but well-manicured garden, drinking lukewarm Chablis from expensive crystal glasses, one of the few surviving legacies of a comfortable marriage to a successful antique dealer, and wonder, each in turn, what the world was coming to. At some point during the evening, Helen would discreetly remind her daughter how she'd always warned against marrying a much older man, especially a Gemini, then, true to form, she'd overcook something from the freezer which neither of them would eat.

A fresh breeze rustled through the trees at the edge of the copse as Leo headed back to the house. He gazed up at the web of branches criss crossing the sky in the fading light and wondered where Caroline would be, what she might be doing. Across the field, over to the south and well above the sky line, a misty moon was beginning to take shape.

At about ten thirty Leo turned off the television, rubbed his eyes, poured himself a generous brandy and headed for bed with that morning's newspaper tucked under his arm. After a cool shower he checked his weight, slipped on a black silk dressing gown and arranged three plump, feathery pillows for comfortable reading then stretched himself out on the bed, newspaper neatly folded at the City page.

Property prices, according to `experts' on page seventeen, were continuing to rise in what they enthusiastically described as a positive sign of growing affluence throughout the country. Leo wasn't convinced. Why, if everyone was so wealthy, had the top people's car manufacturer just gone bust? Details of plans to sell off Rolls Royce to the highest bidder, on the opposite page, seemed to suggest that all was not well with the economy.

The newspaper slipped gradually from his hand into a haphazard heap on the floor as his eyes flickered drowsily to a close and he drifted into deep sleep and muddled dreams.

He woke with a start less than an hour later. Paddy barking somewhere, maybe at the top of the stairs. A greeting for Angela perhaps. Not sure. He looked first at the clock on the table next to him, nearly twelve, then to the other side of the bed, still undisturbed. Another short, sharp bark from along the landing. Leo raised himself wearily from the bed, swung his legs out onto the plush carpet, re-tied the tasselled cord on his dressing gown and sat for a while, staring at the crumpled newspaper before folding it flat and placing it on the bedside table.

Out on the landing a single shaft of moonlight shone brightly through the open door of the green room across to the top of the stairs. Paddy, sitting in front of the window on the other side of the room, tail wagging, swishing across the floor like a feather duster, sloped off quietly down the stairs when Leo appeared.

The church clock told a sleepy village it was midnight and Angela was late.

Leo looked out across the garden. The moon, no longer a

perfect circle, not quite round, slipped slowly behind feathery clouds for just a moment then spread a silky film of silver across the lawn, sending the trees into silhouette and small, shapeless creatures scurrying for the shadows. Leo closed his eyes tight and tried to focus on the sharp white glow floating somewhere in the darkness, just in front of him. It quickly faded to a small, hazy blur then burst, silently, into a ball of intense, clear, soothing light which seemed to flood across his mind. And somewhere at its dazzling core, Caroline's voice, softly calling to him.

The latticed windows trembled, vibrating to the throb of a sports car suddenly, noisily, just below him in the drive. Leo's eyes snapped open. Glaring headlights then darkness, the slam of a car door and Angela's footsteps across the drive.

He went back to bed and waited for the welcome light of morning.

Chapter Five

$\mathbf{A}$t exactly nine thirty the following morning the telephone rang out once and then stopped abruptly like a swatted fly. It did it again half an hour later, just as Leo was leaving the house. One ring and then nothing.

Angela tucked a blue checked shirt into embroidered denim jeans and waited at the bedroom window until Leo's car was half way down the drive before going back to the kitchen to call Tim Thatcher.

"Sorry darling," she cooed. "He's only just gone."

"Hold on just one moment." Tim quietly shut the door so he wouldn't be overheard. " What did he say?"

"Not a thing darling." She sat down at the table and sipped the remains of her breakfast coffee. "He was asleep when I got home and we've barely spoken this morning."

"When are you going to tell him then?"

"Soon. Leave it to me. Anyway, he should be with you in ten minutes or so."

Tim checked his watch. "And I should have been at my desk half an hour ago. I'll call you later." He grabbed a brown tweed jacket from the back of the chair, folded it over his arm and headed down stairs to the office.

It had started to drizzle by the time the black Rolls Royce sounded its horn outside Thatchers and Leo stepped out into the road with apologetic waves to the tooting traffic building up behind him. He walked quickly around to the other side of the car, opened the passenger door and waited, green umbrella at the ready, like a doorman at Claridges.

Tim rapped on the window, face somewhat grotesquely distorted through a pane of Victorian bevelled glass, mouthing something, head shaking, gesturing with his left hand, inviting Leo to come inside.

The brass bell danced on its spring and Leo's anxious face

peered around the door. He glanced across to Caroline's empty desk and felt the all too familiar sharp stabbing pain into the centre of his stomach.

Tim pointed to a chair, assured him he'd only be a tick, then picked up the telephone receiver laying in the middle of his blotter and returned to his call, with profuse apologies to whoever it was at the other end of the `phone.

No, he didn't think it would take too long to sell their house if they were prepared to drop the price by a few hundred pounds and, yes, there were quite a few other properties in a similar price band but that wasn't necessarily a bad thing.

Leo waited, mind blank, unthinking, staring at Caroline's chair.

Tim eventually put down the `phone and slumped back in his chair. "Selling houses would be fun if we didn't have clients," he said, slapping a green file firmly closed. "Anyway, we've got a bevy of beautiful houses for you to see today Leo, always assuming Caroline ever finishes fixing her face. She's been in there ten minutes or more."

Blood began to flow again through Leo's veins as his pulse rate slipped effortlessly into top gear and the pain in his stomach faded away, as if by magic.

Caroline appeared in the archway from the back office looking like a seasoned mannequin, waved a hand in silent greeting, stepped elegantly over to her desk and took a small pile of property details from the centre drawer. She turned away for a moment, fiddled with the belt on her white, flared trousers then slipped keys of various shapes and sizes into the pockets of a navy blazer and, with a coy smile, made towards the door.

"Are we ready?" she said cheerfully.

Leo stood up in time to see the traffic warden taping a £2 parking ticket to the windscreen of his car.

"Yes, of course, ready when you are". The brass bell

sounded a happier note as he opened the door wide and followed her to the car. "Where to first?"

"To Mrs Lloyd and the `The Old Coach House', down towards Godalming." Caroline waved two sheets of paper, stapled together with the picture of a wisteria-covered cottage on the front and settled herself in the car. "She's off to Australia to live with her daughter and needs a quick sale."

Leo nodded, tossed the parking ticket into the glove compartment and set off down the high street. "Sorry about last night," he said at once. "I didn't mean to upset you."

Caroline pointed urgently to the road sign. "Take the right hand fork," she said. "Then left at the lights." She quickly checked the directions on the last page before she answered him. "I wasn't upset, really I wasn't."

"But you put the `phone down."

"There was nothing more to say." She leaned forward to check her bearings. "Right at the post box over there."

Leo pulled into the side of the road and stopped the car. "It just sounded a bit strange, far-fetched, meeting in the moon and all that."

"That's why I stopped talking about it." She looked out towards the passing traffic. "It all sounds so ridiculous and dramatic when you put it into words, like one of Paula Maxwell's psychic visions."

"I thought I'd lost you," he said quietly. "That I'd never see you again. One of the worst night's of my life."

"But you almost made it to the moon. You very nearly did it Leo, really."

Leo stared at her. "How would you know that?"

"I was waiting for you." Her face softened into a smile. "Just as I promised, midnight in the moon."

He thought for a moment, trying to remember all the details of the night before. "I'm not too sure what happened to be honest," he said. "I think I heard your voice just before

Angela's car roared into the drive and completely shattered the illusion."

"Everything's an illusion Leo, just everything. But some illusions are more real than others." She looked into his eyes, her head tilted slightly back, inviting him to kiss her.

Leo's arms presented a new and completely unexpected problem. Like a school boy on his first date, he shifted them about awkwardly, finally leaving the left draped uneasily across the back of the seat and the other, now seemingly surplus to requirements, hovering uncertainly in the region of Caroline's thigh. It didn't feel right, not right at all, but it was the best he could manage.

Caroline sensed his embarrassment. She gently touched the side of his face and gave him a reassuring smile.

"I think it's probably impossible to kiss someone who's smiling," he said solemnly.

"Sorry. I'll try to be more helpful," she said, pulling him towards her and kissing him lightly on his lips.

"I wonder," he whispered, having found a use for the redudant right arm. "Can we do this on the moon or would that be asking too much?"

"Not sure. We'll have to see."

The agent's particulars said `The Old Coach House' had a lot of potential, which meant a lot of work was needed to bring it up to scratch. Mrs Lloyd described in detail all the improvements she and Mr Lloyd had planned over the years but never quite got around to doing. There was the small box bedroom, ear-marked as a second bathroom, en suite as well, and the lounge which was going to be extended out across the lawn, near the swimming pool they'd planned in what was now the kitchen garden. The sauna would have been on the right of the apple trees, over by the fence, but what with one thing and another and the school fees and Mr Lloyd's back, which had been a constant worry over the years, the plans were postponed.

Leo explained it wasn't what he had in mind, thanked Mrs Lloyd for her time, complimented her on a cosy home and left with a friendly wave. Then off to open farmland and a converted barn, at least twenty five miles from the coast, improbably named `Home Waters'.

`The Manor', a modest bungalow set tidily in a small garden, crazy paving, multi-coloured plants in plastic tubs beyond a white picket fence, was crossed off the list without troubling his lordship or his lady wife. Agent's particulars, for which Caroline refused to accept any responsibility whatsoever, made no mention of the busy railway line just beyond the garden of an otherwise delightful period cottage. The builder's yard, noisy neighbours to a Victorian farm house, had been totally ignored, along with the pig farm, just along the road from an over-priced chalet style property.

The rain had stopped by the time they reached the last of Caroline's selection of possibilities. No agent's particulars or photographs, just a few rough notes, in Tim Thatcher's hand writing, on a small scrap of paper. It was by far the most expensive of the half dozen properties they'd seen that day and although it was not yet officially on the market the owners had already moved out. Gone to Spain or somewhere.

Off the main Guildford road, about a mile across open common land, then left just past the church and down a long, narrow track, neatly edged with conifers which eventually opened out into a cobbled courtyard in front of a biscuit-coloured house. Two old farm cottages merged into one, modernised and extended but according to the notes, still retaining many of the original old world features.

Leo liked it. It had good vibes. A quick tour, no more than ten minutes and he'd made up his mind. He'd get back and make an offer before anyone else had a chance to see it.

Caroline locked-up the house and they walked back together

to the car. "You certainly move fast when you really want something," she said.

"Perhaps not quite as fast as I'd like." Leo leaned against the roof of the car, quickly jotted down some figures on the back of Tim's notes, stood back and scratched his head. "It's more than I intended to pay," he said, checking his calculations again. "I might have to do a bit of short term borrowing. Nothing serious. Shouldn't really slow things down."

Leo took a last look at the house as they set off back along the track, towards the road. "There's only one big draw back," he said. "If I buy this place I won't have an excuse to spend my time driving around looking at properties with you, will I?"

She grinned. "I suppose you could always look around for two or three more to avoid suspicion."

"Not at these prices. I can't believe how much they've gone up since I bought `Pelham Green Farm House'." Leo checked himself in the rear view mirror and took a deep breath. "There is, of course, another way we could see more of each other."

She tilted her head forward and peered round at him. "And what might that be?"

"We could live together."

He stared straight ahead at the lunchtime traffic, waiting for the response. It wasn't what he'd hoped for. Caroline looked uneasy.

"Live together where?" she asked.

"The place we've just seen. Does it have a name?"

"I think it's called `Brambley Cottage', something like that. You've got the notes." Her voice was now slightly clipped.

Leo unfolded the sheet of paper with one hand and glanced down at the scribbled details. "It looks like `Bramble Cottage' actually, but I think I prefer your name. How do you fancy living at `Brambley Cottage'?"

"Not now," she said immediately. "It's not the right time." Her expression softened as she turned to face him. "I was going to tell you," she said quietly. "I'm going away for a while. Not for long. Back before you know it."

Leo unbuttoned his shirt collar, tugged his tie loose and fanned himself with Tim's notes. "That sounds to me like the brush off."

"I'm sorry, it really wasn't meant to." She reached out for his hand. "`Brambley Cottage'` was a beautiful thought and I'm truly flattered." She hesitated for a moment. "It's just that there are things which must be sorted out before we can be together properly."

"There's a Mr Blanchard somewhere? Is that it?"

"The only Mr Blanchard I've ever known was my father, and he died in 1943. Honestly, there's nobody else involved. Nobody at all."

"Angela's involved."

"Yes of course, there's Angela, but she has nothing to do with this."

"It's private then? Something you'd rather not tell me about."

"It's not private and I'll tell you all about it when the time's right. Promise." She shuffled the handful of property details into a neat pile and perched her sunglasses on the end of her nose as the car turned right at the cross roads and into the high street. "To business," she said. "Are you coming in to talk to Tim about `Brambley Cottage'?"

Leo stopped the car and stared at Thatcher's window. "Tell him I'll call him this afternoon with an offer."

Caroline opened the car door. "See you tonight, in the moon. Don't forget now," she said.

Leo, right hand raised against the glare of the sun, called after her. "Suppose there isn't a moon tonight. Then what?"

"But there will be. Trust me." She blew him a kiss and quickly went inside.

The clock above the chemist's shop on the opposite side of

85

the road said it was one thirty when he turned the car around and set off towards London where an extra long Mercedes, darkened windows, bristling with aerials and antennae, impudently parked in Leo's usual space on the forecourt of The Westbury, sent him searching for small change and a parking meter in nearby Berkeley Square.

Chin raised he struggled with the button on his shirt collar and re-knotted his tie as he walked slowly back along Bruton Street to the office where Claudia Hamilton, glistening in an emerald green satin jacket with padded shoulders, presided over the reception desk during Sara's lunch break.

She pointed with a ball point pen to a pile of pink message slips at the far end of the bamboo counter. "I've been trying to get you on the car `phone," she said. "Couple of urgent calls."

"Hmm, sorry," Leo mumbled. "Must have forgotten to switch it on." He flicked quickly through the pile, pulled out two which seemed slightly more important than the rest and dealt with them almost as soon as he'd settled himself at the desk with a half filled mug of coffee. An hour later, waste bin overflowing with crumpled balls of pink paper, he called Thatcher's and made an £18,000 offer for `Bramble Cottage' to an answering machine. Tim Thatcher's recorded voice crackled an apology for the office being temporarily unattended and assured callers of his personal attention directly he returned.

Leo's bank manager, a small round man with whiskers and a voice like a mewing cat, evasive and noncommittal as always, was sorry but he couldn't approve a short term loan for property investment, at least not on the telephone. But he was fairly sure the bank would probably be prepared to accept the deeds to `Pelham Green Farm House' as collateral for borrowing at four per cent above base rate. And, of course, the loan would have to be fully fluctuating, whatever that meant.

Claudia tottered unsteadily into the room, thick platform soled shoes with ankle straps adding a full two inches to her height, baggy trousers billowing around her ankles like two shiny green spinnakers. Her outfit reminded Leo of the `tarty' styles women wore in the 1940's, during the War. But then fashion was never completely original and usually amounted to little more than an inferior rehash from another time altogether.

She stood in front of the desk, slightly pensive, cuddling her elbows. "I've arranged for a dozen or so of the girls to tour the photographic studios next week," she said. "Show their portfolios, present themselves in the flesh so to speak."

Leo nodded his approval. "Great idea. I think all the girls should have a go at it from time to time. Let's make it a rule."

"Good. That's what I thought." She started back towards the door, hands thrust into her jacket pockets, half looking back over her shoulder. "By the way," she said. "Would it be OK if Lucy came to the office with me next week? She's got her own tray."

Leo looked up at her, eyes narrowed. "Who's Lucy, a waitress?"

"No, she's a Siamese cat. There'll be nobody in the flat next week to look after her while I'm at work." Claudia bit her bottom lip and waited for his reaction.

"What's the tray for?"

"It's her loo," she said, lowering her voice. "Where she goes to the toilet. But there's no smell. Honest."

Leo closed his eyes, shook his head slowly. "Thanks. That's a bit more information than I really needed."

"Is that a 'yes' then?"

"Only if Lucy and her tray stay out of sight – and smell." He ran his fingers wearily through his hair. "And before you disappear, would you get me the deeds to my house? I think they're in a red folder, back of the safe."

"Right away," she said. "And thanks."

She returned after twenty minutes with a red folder and the afternoon post which she placed, in two neat piles, in front of him.

Philip Cornwall. The name listed on the title deeds, immediately before his own, brought back the memory. Obnoxious little man, lank greasy hair, bad breath. Always saying "to *be perfectly honest"*, which he never was. He'd been a problem from the day Leo first saw `Pelham Green Farm House'. A difficult man to deal with, changed his mind all the time and then, on contract day, asking for another £2,000. Fat chance. Leo told him where to go and no more was said about it but the name still rankled and there it was in black and white, Philip Cornwall, followed by the date he'd bought the house, August 1957. Leo casually traced his finger up the page to the previous owner. Jonathan Swabey. According to the deeds, Swabey had sold the house to Cornwall fourteen years earlier having apparently owned it since 1946, when he bought it from......Leo's heart hammered against the inside of his chest. He stared at the page, eyes transfixed on the name ....Caroline Blanchard. July 1943. And immediately above that entry, another Blanchard ....Edwin Blanchard. May 1932.

Edwin Blanchard	**May 1932**
Caroline Blanchard	**June 1943**
Jonathan Swabey	**December 1946**
Philip Cornwall	**August 1957**
Leo Gannesh	**March 1970**

Leo sank back into the chair and slowly ran it all through his mind. 1943, the year Caroline had said her father died. She'd have been no more than three or four years old, much too young to appear on the title deeds of a house. And anyway, she would surely have mentioned it.

He grabbed the telephone directory, quickly flicked to the B's Blackwood, Blaine, Blair, Blakelock, Blanchard. There were at least forty of them in the London area, four of them with the initial C. He called Directory Enquries and asked them to locate a Caroline Blanchard, somewhere in the south of England and, no, he didn't have an exact address but it was somewhere in the Home Counties, possibly Surrey. They couldn't help, not without more details. Far too many C. Blanchards listed in the South East.

Almost certainly a coincidence then. Yes it had to be. Leo telephoned Caroline to tell her about her namesake at `Pelham Green FarmHouse' but again reached Tim's crackled apology and his previous invitation to leave a message. This time Leo didn't bother. He called a few more times from the car on his way home through the London traffic and made one last attempt at six thirty, just before he parked at the back of 'The Kings Oak'. There was still no reply.

Tim Thatcher, seated royally beside the empty fireplace in his favourite Windsor chair, holding court with a small group of locals, looked up as Leo perched himself on a stool at the bar. He raised his glass in welcome then leaned across the small round table to slap an elderly gentlemen enthusiastically on the back, whispered a parting comment which brought bursts of laughter and made his way slowly across the room, drink in hand, to were Leo was sitting.

"Give that man a glass of Champagne," he called to an unseen barman. "And another for me."

Leo swivelled round to face him. "Celebration?"

"But of course." He leaned heavily against the bar, one foot resting on 'the brass rail below. "They've accepted your offer for `Bramble Cottage'. Called me back from Spain almost immediately."

"Oh! I wasn't sure you'd get my message," said Leo. "Never really trusted answering machines."

"Yes, sorry about that." Tim threw his head back and finished his drink. "One of those days. Out and about most of the afternoon I'm afraid."

"Anyway, a toast," said Leo as two glasses of chilled Champagne, misty with condensation, appeared on the bar in front of them. "To you Tim and your delightful assistant. Thank you both for finding me `Bramble Cottage'."

"Former delightful assistant," said Tim raising his glass. "But cheers all the same."

Leo's hand tightened its grip on the cold, damp glass. "Former?" he repeated quietly. "Where's she gone?"

"Not too sure myself." Tim shrugged and emptied his glass. "Off on a sabbatical as far as I can make out," he said, signalling to the barman for more drinks. "All a bit airy fairy really. One day she's looking for a house, next day a job, and the day after that she's off on some kind of trip. Mind you, she always said she wouldn't be staying long"

"Will she be back?" Leo glanced casually around the bar trying to appear disinterested. "I mean, did she say if she'd be coming back at some point?"

"Not in so many words she didn't, but I wouldn't be surprised. She seemed sorry to leave."

Leo took his diary from an inside pocket and laid it on the bar, creased open at a blank memo page. "Do you have her address?" he said, clicking a ball point pen into action.

"Sorry, she never told me." .

"What about a P45, some kind of employment record?"

Tim fidgeted uneasily. "Look," he said quietly. "I paid her in cash but she gave it straight back and asked me to donate it to charity." He stared down at the blank page in Leo's diary. "Caroline was a most unusual woman and I really don't have all the answers to your questions. Is all this important?"

He shook his head. "Not really. I just wanted to ask her if she'd ever lived at `Pelham Green Farm House'. There's a Caroline Blanchard mentioned on the deeds, back in 1943."

"Probably a relative. Obviously couldn't be her - not in '43."

"No, obviously not." Leo ordered another round of drinks.

"So I suppose you'll be looking for a new assistant?"

Tim moved closer, pulled up a bar stool and sat down. "Funny you should mention that," he said. "You see I was thinking of asking Angela; that's if you wouldn't mind of course."

"Mind? Why should I mind?"

"Oh, no reason really. It's just that Angela seemed to think you might not like the idea of her working."

"You've already asked her then?"

Tim took a sip of Champagne. "Well yes actually," he said. "I think she was going to tell you about it."

"I'm sure she will." Leo raised his glass. "So then, another toast. To Tim and his delightful new assistant."

They clinked glasses. Tim placed a friendly hand on Leo's shoulder and proposed a toast. "To the three of us," he said as they both turned to face the bar.

Paula Maxwell, cigarette in her right hand, elbow on the bar, permitted herself a wry smile. "Wonderful news," she said coolly. "I'm sure Angela will just love it, eh Tim?"

Tim ignored her. He quickly looked away towards the chattering group on the other side of the room then turned back to Leo.

"Best be off to the rest of the knights at the round table, care to join us?"

"Not right now thanks," said Leo. "Some other time perhaps."

"As you like." Tim made his way back to the Windsor chair, puffed up the red cushion and sat down, legs outstretched in front of him.

Paula's gold bracelets jangled against the Champagne bottle as she refilled Leo's glass. She stared at him as she drew hard on her cigarette. "I suppose the other girl's gone then," she asked.

"Apparently."

"Doesn't surprise me. Will-o'-the-wisp."

"What do you mean?"

"I'm not sure what I mean." She crushed the end of her cigarette into the ash tray. "But there's something odd about her."

Leo thought for a moment, slid his glass to one side and leaned forward to speak. "Can I ask you something?" he said quietly. "If you were to look up at the moon tonight, then close your eyes, concentrate on the little white dot and try to visualise someone, anyone, do you think you might eventually see them?"

Paula shook her head. "You'd perhaps see the memory of them, merely the picture you carry in your mind."

"But have you heard of people actually meeting each other, talking together?"

She frowned. "What are you up to?" she asked. "You're talking about astral travel."

"Am I?" He slid his drink back in front of him, drew a little face on the misty glass with his finger and watched the tiny tears of condensation trickle down the stem. "I didn't know it had a name. Question is, can it be done?"

"Some people might say so."

"And you Paula, what would you say?"

"I'd say it *could* be done but I'd question whether or not it *should* be done." She lifted his glass, wiped away the trail of damp with a cloth, and set it back down in front of him. "It's dangerous," she said. "Don't get involved."

"Dangerous? How can it be dangerous to stare at the moon? They're planning to drive some kind of buggy up there next month. Now that's what I call dangerous."

Paula slowly shook her head and sighed. "Astronauts are professionals. They know the risks. You're an amateur with no idea what you're getting into."

"I didn't say I was getting into anything," he said, standing up to go.

"You didn't have to," she said. "And, by the way, the drinks were on the house."

Leo ignored her, reached for his back pocket and took out a wad of £5 notes.

"On the house," she repeated firmly then turned quickly away, waved her hand dismissively behind her and moved off down the bar to serve another customer.

He walked towards the door, glancing back as he opened it. "Thanks," he called out. "I'll be careful."

"Not just careful, be clever Leo. Don't do it at all."

The pile of reclaimed rustic bricks stacked near the garage block appeared noticeably smaller from the end of the drive. Leo accelerated up to the house, stopped the car and stared through the open window across to the empty pallet. He went quickly inside, followed the trail of plastic sheets which covered the carpet leading to the lounge and flung open the door. An ugly, gaping scar on the wall immediately opposite, jagged wounds grey and damp with fresh cement, where glass mosaic once sparkled with life. And growing upwards and outwards across the wall, a rustic scab of bricks beginning to cover the barbaric surgery.

The clock, dusty and dirty on the window ledge, cement specks on its face, had stopped at one thirty. Leo picked it up, wiped it with his handkerchief and started down the hall towards the kitchen. He stopped near the foot of the stairs. "What have you done you mindless bitch?" he yelled at the ceiling. "Come and tell me what you think you've bloody well done here."

"Is that you darling?" Angela's voice, faint but cheerful, almost lost in the sound of running water. "I'm up here."

Leo climbed the stairs slowly but deliberately, paused at the top, some deep breaths, a futile attempt to calm himself, then along the landing to the bedroom and through, into the

93

bathroom where Angela, hair held back in a red towel, eyes closed, lay motionless in the bath.

"Be a darling. Pass me a towel," she whispered, eyes tightly closed as if she might have soap in them, right arm reaching out blindly.

He placed the clock down carefully beside the hand basin, took down a large towel from the glass shelf and placed it in her hand.

She glanced at him then quickly turned away. "You look tired darling," she said. "Why don't you have a quiet bath before dinner?"

Leo's eyes narrowed. "What have you done with it?"

She pulled the red towel from her head, swished her hair from side to side. "It's gone," she snapped. "Gone for good."

He grabbed her arm. "Gone where?"

"To auction."

Leo, struggling to compose himself, slowly loosened his grip and sat down on the edge of the bath. "I want you to dry yourself and dress now Angela," he said in a surprisingly calm voice. "Then I want the names and telephone numbers of everyone involved in today's act of vandalism." He stood up, checked himself in the mirror and adjusted his tie. "After that I want everything back, just the way it was, the way it was meant to be. Do I make myself clear?"

"Perfectly. But what about what I want?" she screamed.

"And what exactly do you want Angela?" He picked up the clock and walked back into the bedroom.

"I want a divorce."

Leo stood for a while, silent, in front of the open wardrobe, carefully selected a couple of suits which he placed on the bed with half a dozen neatly folded shirts and a handful of ties, then collected his electric razor and toothbrush from the bathroom.

"Did you hear me?" Angela, tight lipped, a towel draped loosely around her, pumped a generous mist of perfume across her shoulders from a chunky square bottle. "I said I want a divorce."

"So you did. And you shall have one my darling," he said quietly. "Meanwhile I shall move my things into the green bedroom."

Her eyes flashed. "Can you simply write-off ten years of marriage, just like that? No argument, nothing?"

"What's to argue about? For once in our lives we agree."

Angela followed him into the bedroom. "Funny, I thought you loved me," she said.

"I thought so too but it just shows you how wrong you can be. Love is quite a different thing."

"Is there somebody else?"

He turned to face her, clothes bundled haphazardly in his arms. "I sincerely hope so," he said. "But I'm not altogether sure."

"How long have you known her?"

"I think maybe I've always known her."

Angela swaggered over to the dressing table, sat down purposefully and spoke to the irate woman in the mirror. "I don't want to hear any more of this," she said. "Not another word." She waited for Leo to leave the room then reached for a crimson lipstick and set to work on a brand new, shameless face.

Tie discarded, shirt sleeves rolled to the elbow, shoes kicked carelessly to one side, Leo positioned a green wicker chair by the open French doors, looking out across the garden and relaxed with a very large whisky and soda poured over ice into a long glass. He lay back comfortably, crossed his legs, quickly dismissed a fleeting notion that four glasses of Champagne might not happily blend with Scotland's finest malt and resolved to think about absolutely nothing, not a thing, sod all.

Angela appeared behind him and gently touched his

shoulder. "I'll ring the builder about the fireplace," she said quietly but apologetically. "They can collect it from the auction rooms in the morning."

He nodded and tilted his head round to face her. "Going out?" he asked.

"Just a quick meal."

"Right. See you later then."

"Don't suppose I'll be too late." She turned to go then paused. "We can still at least be friends can't we Leo? I mean, we don't have to hate each other do we?"

He swivelled round in the chair and stared at the long black hair, pulled back tight into a pony tail, the white crocheted dress showing off the sun-tanned legs. "I could never hate you," he said pensively. "And I guess you could never really hate me, not as much as Art Deco fireplaces anyway."

A weak, sad smile softened her face before she looked quickly away. "Something in my eye," she said, dabbing it with a tissue. "Well I'll be off then." Her quavering voice belied the confident swagger towards the door

Leo turned back towards the garden. "Have you known him long?" He raised his glass to his lips and waited for the reply.

"No, not long. Not really."

"Do you love him?"

She laughed, a silly pretend laugh, the sort that fools nobody, closed the door quietly behind her and stood, for a moment, quietly in the hall. Leo listened until the hum of her car had faded into the distance, freshened his drink and settled back in the chair.

A cold wet nose nudging his arm, a craggy paw rasping across his hand, then the muffled, throaty bark. Leo opened his eyes to the late evening gloom, hand wearily extended towards the sound, pulled himself free of the wicker chair and stepped unsteadily into the garden and the refreshing chill of the night air. He checked his watch - ten to twelve. Standing perfectly still in the silence, hands in pockets, quite alone, his shadow barely reaching the geraniums at the edge of the terrace, he wondered how once, perhaps even yesterday, he'd imagined he was somehow important. Right now, here, tonight, he knew nobody was important except to somebody else. And, for him at least, there was nobody.

Caroline, somewhere of course, God knows where, perhaps with someone else. The moon, floating across the pool, bright, dazzling even, just as she'd promised. He threw back his head, gazed upwards through heavy eyes. "See you tonight in the moon," she'd said. "Don't forget."

Leo stepped back to the shadows of the room. Squiffy or maybe just tired. Not sure. Tipsy probably. Champagne and whisky didn't go well together after all. Pity but, like he and Angela, best on their own. Separate, apart.

A flood of moonlight reached the open doors and washed across the room. What was it Paula had called it? `Dangerous', that's what she said. `Don't do it'. Silly cow. He settled himself in the chair and stared back defiantly at the soft white glow.

Blinded, just for a moment, his eye lids flickered. Someone, a woman, standing in the centre of the rose arch at the top of the steps leading away from the pool to the tall willow. Motionless for a fleeting second before she turned and walked slowly across the lawn towards the house then stopped at the edge of the terrace, waiting for him in the half light. He started towards her, moving closer until the features were clear.

Caroline, arms outstretched towards him, more beautiful than any memory, any picture in the mind. She was here, now, his special someone, the somebody else who made him important.

Fragile, silver notes from a distant piano filtered softly through the jasmine, sound and scent magically distilled into one, a heady elixir drifting across the summer night to enchant the senses and seduce reality itself into sweet submission. And

Caroline, the very essence of the hypnotic, misty spell, fading back towards the shadows, enticing him, daring him to follow. But then gone.

Chapter Six

Harley Street was only a stone's throw from the Leo Gannesh model agency but, like a lemming to a cliff, the taxi driver had raced full throttle towards the nearest traffic jam and wedged himself firmly into the centre, clocking up an extra fifteen minutes just off Hanover Square and making Leo even later than he already was for the appointment with Doctor Petigrew.

He ran a shaky hand through neatly parted hair and made an effort to ignore the rhythmic throb of the bongo drums, somewhere in the centre in his swollen, aching brain. A humdinger of a hangover, no more than he deserved after last night's binge, but he could live with that. What worried him were the stomach pains. Not so much stomach pains really, more of a sharp stabbing sensation on the right hand side which had started during the night.

The doctor, who spoke very quietly and mostly looked out of the window, told him to strip down to his underpants and lay down, face up, on the examination couch before pressing cold, hard finger tips into his belly.

"I had a few drinks last evening," Leo confessed cheerfully. "May have overdone it perhaps. You know how it is, a couple of glasses of Champagne, then a few Scotches." The words trailed off into a feeble laugh.

Doctor Petigrew peered across the top of half spectacles, expressionless, shook his head dismissively and returned to his notes without a word.

"Could be the old liver I suppose." Leo tapped his fingers on the sides of the couch and gazed up at the ceiling waiting for a response.

The doctor felt his pulse. "Very possibly," he murmured into his watch. "Hardly beneficial for your heart either. Ticker's OK." Leo slapped his chest with a loose fist. "No problems there. Had it checked only recently."

Doctor Petigrew stepped back to his desk, positioned the lamp over his notes and sat down. He removed his glasses. "You can get dressed now," he said.

Leo raised himself up on one elbow and stared across at the hunched figure behind the desk. "What's the verdict then?" he enquired casually, swinging his legs to the floor.

Petigrew looked up, a sickly, caustic smile on his lips. He blinked slowly as he spoke. "The verdict, Mr Gannesh, is that a man of your age must moderate his drinking if he hopes to maintain reasonable heart and liver function for the remainder of his life."

Leo nodded, sat down on a hard wooden chair and looked across to the building opposite and the girl at the second floor window, pale blue dress, shoulder length auburn hair, high cheek bones, almost Caroline. He slipped on his shirt, quickly buttoned up the front and reached for his trousers. "What about hallucinations?" he asked casually. "I mean, could you start to imagine things?"

"Intoxication always diminishes control of the faculties and reason, sometimes even the mind." The doctor, now more serious, demanded direct eye contact. "Some people occasionally see things," he said pointedly.

"That's what I thought."

Leo's attention strayed across the room to a dismembered torso displayed on top of a small cupboard near the window. Over-sized liver, plump and smooth like a generous helping of chocolate blancmange, squashed in tightly between a swirling pile of pink entrails and the anaemic stomach wall of an apparently sexless being with a cut-away plaster belly. He finished dressing as fast as he could manage, slipped a prescription for some kind of tablets into his wallet, then back down the wide, sweeping staircase to the front door. Outside in the morning sunshine he promised himself to avoid spirits, at least for a while.

A leisurely walk back to the office, a short stop for a strong black coffee and the bongo rhythms started to fade. By lunchtime Leo felt almost human, ready to rationalise the hazy recollections of Caroline Blanchard's midnight visit.

Too much to drink, far too much. Simple as that really. And it wasn't the first time. There was that balmy summer night in 1932. Three young men, too many brandies, and a fractured finger after diving from a grassy bank into the A40 near Oxford, glistening and cool like the River Thames, every bit as real as Caroline last night in the garden but just an impenetrable, unforgiving, rain-soaked stretch of road.

The afternoon sun slipped behind tall buildings and loitered over Hyde Park putting Bond Street into shadow and cooling the day for the women with a purpose, promenading and poised, clusters of expensive shopping bags gripped tightly by jewelled fingers, the scent of excess in the air, a fragrant potpourri of extravagance, lavishly distilled from the very finest of the world's most exclusive labels. The unmistakable smell of wealth.

Leo glanced at his reflection in the shop window as he passed. There was a definite stoop. He straightened up, shoulders back, and joined a small queue in the chemists to collect Doctor Petigrew's pills, small, white and round, just like aspirin but considerably more expensive. Then back to Guildford with a plan of action to find out more about Caroline Blanchard, or at least the Caroline Blanchard named on the deeds to 'Pelham Green Farm House'.

A pasty-faced woman at the Registrar of Births, Deaths & Marriages, lank, greasy hair, no sign of make-up, pushed grey cardigan sleeves up beyond bony elbows and made every effort to be as uncooperative as possible in the short time still available before the offices closed for the day at four thirty. A name wasn't enough. She couldn't confirm the details of anyone's death, not without the place and the date of the demise.

Leo stared at the wall in front of him beyond the wooden counter, an official wall, half green half cream, a narrow blue line dividing the two. He guessed that this Caroline Blanchard would probably have inherited 'Pelham Green Farm House' on the death of Edwin Blanchard in June 1943, so there was a name, a date and a place. The pasty face reddened as he filled-in the form, the cardigan sleeves forced higher up the arms, more urgent sidelong glances at the clock to the right of the door before she he stalked off huffily down the corridor.

She returned after ten minutes. There was no record of the death of an Edwin Blanchard at 'Pelham Green Farm House' in June 1943 but she'd taken the trouble to see if he'd died at the local hospital. She handed Leo a copy death certificate and looked back at the clock. Twenty past four.

Leo laid the paper on the counter and traced the hand-written scrawl with his finger. Edwin Blanchard, Died june 2nd, 1943. Age 55. Cause of death cerebral abscess. Informant Caroline Blanchard, daughter.

He turned to leave but stopped at the door and thought for a moment. This Caroline Blanchard would be at least fifty today, maybe even more, if she'd been old enough to be named on her father's death certificate nearly thirty years ago. By now she might even be dead herself. Obviously not *his* Caroline Blanchard.

The lady behind the counter, cardigan now hanging, limp, grey and lifeless on a hook near a metal filing cabinet on the other side of the room, slipped her arms into a pink bolero jacket, fastened two silver buttons and prepared to leave.

Leo ran his tongue anxiously across his lips and stepped slowly back towards the counter, hands clasped together, earnestly, in front of him. "Before you go," he said in his most polite and appealing voice, "could I just ask you to look-up one more name for me?"

She blinked impatiently, sighed, pointed towards the clock. "We're meant to close now," she said. "Half past four."

Leo nodded. "I realise it's a great imposition but I'd be eternally grateful." He glanced at the ink-stained fingers tapping irritably on the counter while he filled-in the second form. A long shot but worth a try.

It was nearly twenty to five when she returned with the death certificate. *Caroline Blanchard. Died November 12th 1946. Age 31.* This Caroline Blanchard, it said, 'took her own life' twenty five years ago, the year the house was sold to Jonathan Swabey. Definitely not his Caroline Blanchard then. But who?

A suicide meant an inquest and that meant local newspaper coverage. With any luck the *Surrey Advertiser* would have reported the details at the time. Leo reversed out of the car park and made a dash for the Reference Library before it closed.

Less than thirty minutes later the library's photo-copier purred into life, sending a narrow shaft of bright yellow light skimming across the wall of an otherwise dismal room. It spat out one single sheet of paper into a plastic tray then clicked to a stop. The young girl asked Leo for ten pee.

He leaned against the car, one hand in his trouser pocket, and read the cutting for the third time. Just a few paragraphs, not many words, no pictures. Local artist Caroline Blanchard, 31, died from an overdose of sleeping tablets early on the morning of November 12th 1946. The coroner said no note had been found but the circumstances of the death were not suspicious. He said she had taken her own life. There were no known relatives and her will left everything to charity, including more than 30 oil paintings, mainly portraits.

Leo felt uncomfortable, as if he'd been rummaging through someone's private life, prying into their past. It didn't seem right. He stood quietly in front of the waste bin outside the library, slowly ripped up the sad testimony to a short and tragic life and left it in peace with the discarded packets, wrappers and empty bottles.

A white builders' truck passed him near the entrance to 'Pelham Green Farm House', two men in overalls slouching in the back with the sand and cement, legs outstretched, arms draped over the sides, motionless like rag dolls tossed carelessly into a box. And at the front of the house, two clear indentations where brick pallets had stood earlier in the day.

Milly appeared in the porch, looked quickly across to Leo's car then went back inside, leaving the front door wide open and the smell of fried onions drifting invitingly across the drive towards him. He followed it down the hall and into the kitchen, poured himself a glass of water and shook out two of Doctor Petigrew's tablets from a small brown bottle.

"What are they for?" Milly adjusted the top of her apron and nodded her head twice, adding a sense of urgency to the question.

Leo refilled the glass. "Liver," he said in between gulps.

"Nothing wrong with your liver," she assured him confidently. "I can tell by your eyes."

"I'm pleased to hear it," said Leo. "But I'll just finish these off to please the doctor." He rattled the bottle, slipped it into his pocket and started back towards the hall, then stopped and turned at the door. "Not one of your usual days today is it Milly?"

"No. It. Is. Not." Four short words delivered like hammer blows. Milly, obviously not happy with the arrangements, wearing her 'taken-forgranted' expression, speaking in the 'put-upon' voice she used so often. "Mrs Gannesh rang me this morning," she said. "Asked me to look out for the builders and cook you some dinner."

"Oh, I see." Leo smiled weakly. "What am I having?"

She opened the fridge door, took a plate from the top shelf

and set it down on the kitchen table. "Liver," she announced blandly then, as something of an after thought, "with onions."

Leo looked at it, cold and lifeless on the plate, like the chocolate blancmange on Dr Petigrew's plaster torso but much smaller. A slight twinge in his side. Probably the tablets kicking-in.

"Right," he said, "I'll just go and see what the builders have been up to."

He poked his head round the door to the lounge, uneasy, apprehensive. Leaning up against the wall, ready for fixing, the mirrored mosaic fireplace, grubby finger prints all over the place but back, back where it belonged, reunited with the room.

"I'll be off now then." Milly's voice echoed in the hall. "Your dinner's in the oven, red casserole dish." She slowly nudged the door open, leaned forward and stared cautiously around the room without venturing in. "Everything all right in there is it?" she said. "I cleaned up as much as I could."

Leo brushed himself down, quietly closed the door behind him and kissed her on both cheeks. "Everything's perfect Milly, just perfect. Thank you."

She smiled and turned to go. "Oh, I nearly forgot, a lady called. She said not to forget your appointment. Some pub or another. Tell him I'll see him in The Moon, she said. That was it."

"Did she leave a telephone number?" Leo asked impatiently.

"It was a very bad line. Difficult to hear everything she said but I don't think so. I'd have written it down if she had." Milly said goodbye to the dog, patted him gently on the head and made towards the front door. "I'll miss my bus if I'm not careful," she said. The door slammed behind her and she hurried off down the drive.

Leo gave his dinner to the dog, produced an impromptu omelette, chopped mushrooms, sliced spring onions, and laid

105

himself a place at the kitchen table with a bottle of chilled Chablis and one of his favourite wine glasses with gold round the rim. He looked across to the empty chair opposite then down at his plate. It seemed wrong for one person, alone, isolated and detached, to be making all this fuss. And, anyway, he wasn't very hungry. He scraped his plate into the waste bin under the sink and went to bed, leaving the washing up in the sink.

Delicate filigree hands on the Cartier clock at last dawdled around to midnight, twelve tinkling chimes followed by silence. Shadowy clouds crept out from the darkness of the sky, crawled across the fragile, hazy burst of moonlight above the trees beyond the open bedroom window and slowly blotted it out. And then black.

Leo pushed another cushion behind his head and lay perfectly still on top of the bed, staring out into the dark. The dim, pink glow of Guildford somewhere in the distance, above it a single star, a glimmer of light from within the shifting cloud. He closed his eyes, filled his mind with Caroline, and waited for the moon.

A soft breeze whispered from the open window, blowing the bedroom door to a gentle, muffled close and leaving the scent of jasmine in the still night air. Leo sat up, blinked his eyes open to brilliant moonlight and stared around the room. He quickly tightened the black silk dressing gown around him, opened the door and stepped out onto the landing, sending a narrow shaft of light along the wall and a flurry of shadows across the staircase and down to the hall below.

Through the half open door to the lounge, the faint sound of unfamiliar music. A pale, cool light on someone just beyond the door; Caroline, waiting by the window. Leo stood, unmoving, in the doorway. The mirrored mosaic fireplace, back where it was meant to be, dominating the room, the Cartier clock, magnificent, on top, but everything else different, changed. Paintings, lots of them, hanging high on the walls, and above the fireplace the portrait of a man.

Caroline moved slowly towards him, arms outstretched, smiling, just as she had the night before.

He felt the soft folds of the long silky white dress as his hand brushed lightly across her shoulder and found the back of her neck, fingers sliding into her hair. She seemed very real. Their lips touched for just a moment before he drew back. "This is crazy," he whispered. "Am I dreaming or wishful thinking?"

Caroline looked up into his eyes and touched his cheek with soft slender fingers. "Dreams and wishes are real when the time is right." She slid her arms around his waist. "And this is our time Leo. Our special time to be together."

He hesitated, looked around the room for something, anything which might make sense of it all and waited, expecting the illusion to fade into nothing, like before. But it didn't. "Where the hell is this?" he heard himself call out.

"Where all the best stories begin of course. Once upon a time." She took his hand, led him to the open window. New shadows in the garden, unfamiliar silvery shapes in the moonlight.

Across the lawn a tall oak tree, stubby trunk neatly encircled by a low stone seat and, to the right, the statue of a woman, bronze perhaps, one arm raised gracefully to heaven, dress swirling, dancing. The swimming pool, gone; instead a small round summer house, thatched roof, neat latticed windows, wooden tables and chairs arranged outside.

"Complete tranquillity," she said quietly, wrapping her arm firmly around his. "Undisturbed calm?"

The painting above the fireplace worried him. "Who's that?" he asked, nodding towards the arrogant face on the canvas.

Caroline turned slightly, looking back across the room. "It's my father. And that's my mother, facing him." She pointed to

107

the portrait of a woman on the opposite wall. "Do you think I look like her?"

"Your mother's a beautiful woman, if that's what you mean."

"She's not here now," She said, her voice softer, barely audible. "The blitz. It was a friend's house in London. Nobody survived."

He gently squeezed her hand then turned back almost at once towards the painting above the fireplace. "What about your father?"

"He's not here either."

"And you Caroline?" he asked with a new urgency in his voice. "Are you here?

She wrinkled the petite freckled nose and moved back towards the window. "We're both here Leo. You and I and everything else in my fairy story. It's my wonderful once upon a time."

"I'd like to hear your story if it makes some kind of sense of all this."

"It's not just one story Leo." Caroline turned her face towards the moonlight, looking out towards the oak tree. "We've had lots of stories. One day you'll remember them all." She sat down on the floor, leaning against the wall under the window ledge, knees drawn up to her chin, arms wrapped around her legs like a small child.

Leo, crouching in front of her, gently lifted her head. "It said she took her own life on the death certificate," he said quietly. "Who was she?"

"Just a silly, disillusioned woman on the wrong side of thirty who imagined love had passed her by. Too impetuous to wait for her soul mate." She swallowed hard and turned away.

"And the woman I've fallen in love with twenty five years later? Who is she?"

She turned back to face him, smiling through tearful eyes.

"Oh she's the same disillusioned woman, impetuous as ever, looking back at something that should have been, wishing she hadn't been so silly."

"But what about all this?" Leo looked around the room. "What is it?"

She wiped a slender finger across moist eye lids. "It's just a snap shot of another time," she said softly. "Our time Leo, but only a picture, no longer real." She looked up at him. "Can you understand?"

He took her hands, pressed his lips gently against her cheek. "These past few weeks weren't just a snapshot," he said. "They were real, you were real."

"Almost real Leo. So very nearly real."

"But if not completely real, then what?"

"Only a brief and fragile illusion, my darling," she whispered. "The shape and form of a woman who once was real, once upon a time." The deep sadness in her eyes began to fade as if a great hurt was being taken from her, washed away leaving her reconciled, calm. Her face slowly softened into a delicate smile, her voice more hushed. "I'm sorry. It was just a fleeting vision of the Caroline Blanchard you should have met, loved, twenty five years ago."

Leo rose slowly to his feet and stepped backwards towards the door. "Then it was a cruel and unforgivable deception. A taste of the unobtainable with a woman who's gone forever."

"Not forever Leo." Her eyes followed him across the room. "I'll be back, we both will. And next time we'll be together. There'll be a new story with a happy ending. I promise."

"What about this story? How does it end?"

"You know how Caroline Blanchard's story ends," she said, resting her head back against the wall. She paused, her face more serious, the smile gone. "When you choose the ending for your story we can slam the book closed, put it back on the shelf and start our new story, together."

109

"Just like that?"

"It's that simple Leo. You choose."

He stood motionless in the door way, uncertain what to say. "You mean kill myself," he said eventually. "Take my own life, as you did?"

"That's one ending." She stood up and walked slowly towards him, her eyes fixed firmly on his. "One quick and easy way to obtain the unobtainable," she said.

"What shall I do then? Wait for my heart to give out?" Leo forced a feeble laugh. "Perhaps it will be my liver, it's been playing up lately. Who knows, I could get knocked down by a bus."

"It's important to be the master of your own destiny," she said. "Better to take control than let fate rule your life."

He didn't answer.

The first cold light of dawn sent a faint misty glow across the early morning sky. Caroline, silhouetted dimly against the open window, fading with the shadows, her voice more distant. "It's your choice Leo," she called. "Make it soon, for me."

Sunlight percolated through the trees like honey dripping from a silver spoon, chasing the hazy impressions of the night from the room, and sending a shimmering glow across the mirrored mosaic fireplace, still leaning up against the wall, ready for fixing. Leo looked around at the muddled disorder of broken bricks and builder's debris. Under the open window where Caroline had sat, two cement bags, dusty grey powder spilling out across the floor. He tightened the tasselled cord around the black silk dressing gown, clicked the door shut behind him and went back to bed.

The sound of drilling woke him from a brief but dreamless sleep soon after ten. Leo wriggled himself straight, legs outstretched, hands clasped behind his head, and stared up at the ceiling listening to the sounds of the day. Angela's voice below in the drive, Paddy barking somewhere on the other side of the field and muffled grumblings from workmen clattering about on the back of a lorry near the front door.

He breathed deeply for a few moments, tasting the cool, fresh morning air, then rolled his head lazily towards the chest of drawers on the other side of the room trying to remember if that was where he'd last seen the bright red shirt with black buttons. It was probably with the other neatly folded shirts in the bottom drawer, he decided, maybe a little faded with the years but a shirt with character just the same. He swung his legs lethargically to the floor and made towards the bathroom, emerging ten minutes later invigorated, showered and shaved except for the first shadowy stubble of a new moustache.

The red shirt looked almost as good as when he first bought it in a sale five years earlier, apart from a dark stain, probably wine, on one of the cuffs. Leo carefully rolled both sleeves back to mid forearm, opened three buttons at the neck and checked himself in the wardrobe mirror while he threaded a wide leather belt through the waistband of his black worsted trousers.

He glanced out across the drive towards the Porsche. Angela was bent forward, stretching across the front seats, willowy legs splayed apart on platform shoes, tight denim shorts gripping the curves of her bottom like sticking plaster. She was watched by a tall man in white overalls who leaned casually against three steel girders propped up on the back of the lorry. He slowly lit a cigarette with cupped hands, blew smoke in her general direction then, head back, flicked the spent match at the car.

"Nice motor," he said, peering over the side of the lorry. "Always fancied one of them meself."

Angela straightened up, tucked the white T-shirt back into her shorts, and turned to face him. "Did you want something?" she asked abruptly.

"I was just saying, nice car you've got there." He sucked

hard on the cigarette and stared at her.

She gave him a piercing look. "Ever driven a Porsche?" she said coldly.

"No, not really.

"Then what makes you think it's a nice car?"

"Well, looks nice dun it."

"Looks aren't everything." She slammed the car door shut and marched purposefully back into the house.

The smell of burnt toast met Leo on the landing and escorted him to the kitchen where Angela was pouring coffee. Two cups.

"One of those for me?" he asked.

"Who else?" She smiled, placed it on the table in front of him and pulled back the chair for him to sit down. "Fancy some toast?"

Leo shook his head. "Not very hungry this morning. Didn't sleep too well."

"Me neither." She sat down opposite him, nudged the sugar bowl across the table.

"I don't take sugar," he said quietly but firmly. "Never have done."

Angela looked away towards the garden. "No, of course you don't. I forgot." She took a sip of coffee, both hands holding the cup to her lips, then turned back to face him. "I'd forgotten that old red shirt too. Suits you."

Leo leaned forward, elbows on the table, hands clasped in front of his chin. "Who is he? I'd really like to know."

"He's a friend, just a friend." She stood up quickly and took her cup and saucer over to the sink. "Let's not do this Leo," she said, turning her attention quickly to something beyond the window.

"Sorry. Didn't mean to pry." He finished his coffee and made towards the door. "I'm off out for a while. See you later perhaps."

She followed him into the hall. "Drive safely," she called out as he reached the front door.

"I always drive safely." He waited, guessing she probably had something more to say.

"It's Tim Thatcher," she said quietly. "Does it help to know?"

"Not really. No." He shut the door behind him and stood for a while in the front porch staring at the ground. Tim bloody Thatcher, he said to himself. He repeated it several times as he slowly crossed the drive to the garage. Tim bloody Thatcher.

Windows and doors were opened wide to the morning at 'The Kings Oak' where the stale smell of last night's cigarette smoke still lingered stubbornly in the air and a solitary vacuum cleaner hummed across a beer stained carpet. Paula Maxwell, ensconced with a calculator at a small round table in the far corner, carefully bagged-up yesterday's takings for the bank and prepared herself for the lunchtime regulars.

Leo looked across to the Windsor chair near the fireplace, the red cushion already puffed-up and waiting for its usual occupant, four or five chairs placed around the table for the faithful entourage, all of them privy, no doubt, to Tim's goings-on.

Paula raised her head but quickly refocused on the narrow strip of white paper which rat-tatted from the top of the calculator out across the table. "What brings you here so early?" she said through a haze from the first cigarette of the day. "We don't open for another hour."

"It's wisdom I'm after, not wine," he said, twisting a bentwood chair around and straddling it like a horse, arms resting across the back.

"You've probably come to the wrong place then. Pub wisdom is not all it's cracked up to be you know."

Leo took a deep breath and moved the chair nearer to the table. "Caroline Blanchard's dead," he whispered.

Paula seemed suddenly rather vague, as if she might be trying to remember something. She tapped her cigarette against the ash tray a few times before she spoke. "How?, she asked. "When did it happen?"

"That's the point. It happened 25 years ago, 1946. Suicide."

She thought for a moment, staring at the table, fiddling with her fringe. "What can she want?" she murmured to herself. "What's she after?"

Leo broke in, his voice calm and measured, his anxious expression telling a different story. "The question is how was it possible Paula? She was here with us. You saw her, we all did. She had a job with Tim bloody Thatcher for Christ's sake."

Paula looked at him, unblinking. "Is it you she wants Leo? Has she told you that?"

He slowly shook his head. "Something like that. I'm really not sure about anything right now:"

Paula stood up and gathered her things together. "All this moon business, it was her wasn't it? I told you it was dangerous."

"Where's the danger?" Leo called after her as she made towards the bar.

She didn't answer but returned in a moment with a dull red book, the word 'Private' scrawled across the front in smudged blue ink. Her finger flicked decisively to a dog eared page near the back where an assortment of slips of paper, postcards and letters were bunched together in a paper clip. She copied the name and address from a white visiting card with an impressive looking crest at the top onto a strip of paper torn from the calculator and handed it to him.

"Get in touch with this man," she said solemnly. "It's important."

Leo read the name out loud. Justin Charlton-Jones. "Who is he?" he asked.

"Someone who knows about these things." Paula slammed

the book shut, wound a thin elastic band around the covers and thrust it under her arm. She stood for a moment, perfectly still, then raised a finger as if she'd just had a particularly bright idea and disappeared into the back, gesturing to Leo to stay where he was.

He checked the address before slipping it into his wallet. Almost certainly one of those stylish terraces just off Sloane Square; treelined avenues of imposing red brick Victorian buildings with elegant tiled steps leading up to high security front doors. The sort of area where people very often had family crests.

"Three o'clock OK?" Paula shouted from the doorway, telephone in her left hand. "He says he could fit you in."

Leo stood up. "Today you mean?"

She nodded impatiently, waiting for his answer.

"I suppose so."

Paula returned to her cigarette and took a last deep, purposeful inhalation. "That's settled then," she said. "All fixed for three. And just you make sure you are there."

He forced a smile. "Still not quite sure how Mr Charlton-Jones is going to help. I mean, what exactly does he do?"

There was a short silence while Paula stared impatiently at the ceiling, head back, eyes fluttering furiously, like a mother with an obstinate child. "He deals with people like Caroline Blanchard," she sighed. "People who aren't quite where they should be."

Paula's words rang in his ears on the drive to London and by the time he parked the car on a meter just off Lower Sloane Street, he'd already begun to dislike Justin Charlton-Jones. The idea of him in some way *'dealing'* with Caroline Blanchard, whatever that meant, simply wasn't on.

The tall, slim man who answered the door and introduced himself as Jonesy was a surprise, much younger than Leo had imagined. Probably early thirties, he decided, with the aristocratic look of a refugee from the French Revolution. Tight black satin trousers tucked into knee-length black leather boots, a white ruffled shirt with billowing sleeves and straight black hair hanging loosely about a suntanned face.

Up one flight of stairs to a large room which looked out over the tops of the trees in the road outside, comfortably furnished with leather arm chairs and couches, velvet cushions scattered haphazardly around, a few laying on the floor in front of a marble fireplace. Jonesy settled himself at a desk near the window and gestured towards a winged chair immediately opposite. Leo sat down and looked across to the oil painting, unframed, hanging just above the desk; a dull, sludgy portrait of a monk.

"Do you know why you're here?" Jonesy asked quietly as if he didn't want anyone else to hear.

"Not really. No." He felt slightly uncomfortable, brushed some imagined specks from his shirt front and self-consciously crossed his legs. "It was Paula's idea actually."

Jonesy stared at him for a few moments before he continued. "Most people come here because they have abnormal and unexplained experiences which deviate from the pattern of their everyday lives. Is that why you're here?"

"I suppose so."

"Then you must try to describe everything that's happened." Jonesy took a pen from a ceramic jug and began writing on a thick pad of pale blue paper. "Start by telling me whether you feel threatened by what has taken place."

Leo switched his attention to the trees beyond the window. "I don't feel threatened," he said. "Confused, certainly, but definitely not threatened."

"And why are you confused?"

"It sounds so bloody ridiculous." He shook his head and slumped back into the chair. "I've fallen in love with a woman who's probably been dead for the past quarter of a century.'"

Jonesy didn't look up. "And is she in love with you?"

"So she says." He glanced up at the painting of the monk before letting his eyes gently close while he answered a steady stream of probing questions from the figure crouched over the desk in front of him.

Tea arrived shortly after five. A pale, willowy girl in a long black dress, deep blue eyes, jet black hair cascading about her shoulders, quickly placed the silver tray on a low table in the centre of the room. She knelt down beside it and carefully arranged two cups and saucers then smiled timidly and hurried off, unspeaking, as quickly as she had arrived.

"We could have something stronger if you would prefer," said Jonesy.

"Tea will be fine." Leo stood up, stretched and stepped forward for a closer look at the portrait. "It's a very interesting picture," he said.

"He's a very interesting soul."

Leo sipped his tea, peering over the rim of the cup. "Have you met him then?"

"Not exactly. He died three hundred years before I was born but we keep in touch."

"How do you do that; keep in touch I mean?"

"Oh he visits me from time to time when I need his advice."

"Like my visits from Caroline Blanchard you mean?"

"Something like that." Jonesy gathered up his notes and sat down on the larger of two green leather Chesterfields, a slightly tense expression slowly relaxing for the first time that afternoon. "You have a very persistent soul mate Mr Gannesh," he said. "Impetuous, impatient, and above all, impassioned."

Leo's eyes strayed back to the painting. "You forget to mention that she's also dead," he said quietly. "Like your monk."

"Caroline Blanchard may be dead but she was only one

117

incarnation of the soul mate you'll meet in many different lives."

"So what exactly has been happening to me over the past few weeks?"

Jonesy poured another cup of tea. "It's complicated," he said. "But I'll try to explain." He sat perfectly still for a moment, deep in thought, then twisted around to face Leo. "The first thing to try to understand is that the woman you met no longer exists in any physical sense. What you saw was a brief but convincing reflection of Caroline Blanchard, the woman she used to be, who'd apparently like you now to end your life as Leo Gannesh and start a new life together as two totally different people."

"Kill myself." Leo stood wearily up and went over to the window, his back to Jonesy. "Be the master of my own destiny, as Caroline put it." He hesitated, looking out over the tree tops. "Paula said you'd know what to do."

"I know what *I'd* do."

Leo frowned, head half turned. "And what's that then?" he asked.

"I'd live the rest of my life as happily as possible, die when my time was done and prepare for a new life when I was good and ready. Suicide isn't one of the natural responsibilities of the soul."

"Is that the extent of your advice Jonesy? I'd rather hoped for something else, a more constructive answer perhaps."

"Then try asking me a constructive question."

Leo shrugged, rubbing his jaw thoughtfully.

"I'll do my best to help you, give you some answers," said Jonesy. "But you must first provide the questions."

"Like what?"

Jonesy slapped his hand down firmly on the arm of the couch, stood up quickly and crossed the room over to the desk. He took a silver flask from one of the side drawers, poured a brown liquid into a small silver cup and offered it to Leo. "Drink this," he said without explanation.

Leo drew back. "What is it?"

"Poison. Don't worry it's very fast and completely painless." Jonesey stood, legs apart, one arm behind his back, the other outstretched, thrusting the silver cup towards Leo's mouth. "Take it."

"Now just hold on a minute." Leo turned, hands waving in front of him. "I don't want your poison," he said through a feeble, faltering laugh.

"Do you want to end your life?" said Jonesy.

"Certainly not".

"Excellent. That's the most important question answered, a decision made." Jonesy threw his head back and drank down the liquid in a single gulp.

"Not poison then?" Leo asked uncertainly.

"Brandy." He replaced the silver cup on the neck of the flask. "In small doses it's rarely lethal."

"You must think me very stupid."

"People in love are very often stupid; it's the most obvious symptom of the condition." Jonesy went back to the couch and sprawled out with his notes, settled into a velvet cushion, eyes firmly shut, finger tips gently stroking the dull green leather. "So sad," he said after a few moments. "She killed herself only a few short weeks before you were destined to meet." He stopped short, quite still, then opened his eyes wide to the ceiling. "A party, Christmas 1946. Yes, that's it. Somewhere in London, a big hotel perhaps."

Leo nodded. "The Arts Council of Great Britain," he said softly. "Launch party."

"It was where you should have met. Two young people, happy, the end of the war." Jonesy slowly turned towards Leo. "Then New Year in Surrey, the farm house, her house, where she lived, where you now live. I think your Caroline

119

Blanchard's drawn you back there to recreate what might have been."

"But she had nothing to do with me buying `Pelham Green Farm House'."

"Are you sure?" Jonesy sat up, reached over for a tin of small, round mints, popped two into his mouth and gestured to Leo to help himself. "Try to take your mind back. How did you find the house?"

Leo thought for a moment. "A colour brochure. It came through the post."

"Who from?"

"The estate agent. Thatchers."

"And they are, of course, in Guildford," said Jonesy. "Where were you living at the time?"

"We had a flat in Chelsea."

"Not exactly local then. In fact miles away. Had you asked other Guildford estate agents to send you property details?"

"I hadn't asked any estate agents to do anything. To be perfectly honest we weren't even thinking of moving."

"So it was a random mailing? Sent to you on the off-chance?"

"I suppose so. I never really thought about it."

"Then please think about it now. Was there a lot of competition for the house, other people who also wanted it?"

"Funnily enough, there wasn't." Leo rested his arm on the mantelpiece, his back to the fireplace. "But hold on a minute, Caroline didn't turn up at Thatchers until a year after I bought the house."

"But she *did* turn up there eventually," said Jonesy. "And that *was* how you met her."

"Does it matter how we met or why I bought the house? What difference does any of it make?"

Jonesy blinked his eyes impatiently. "It makes all the difference in the world my friend. Believe me." He pushed a cushion to one side, patted the seat of the couch lightly with his hand. "I'd feel more comfortable if you'd sit down," he said, his voice noticeably more hushed. "Next to me, here."

Leo quickly checked his watch, sighed. "Look I think I've taken up enough of your time already. Is there anything else you can tell me?"

"I can tell you she's not alone in this." Jonesy declared. "There's someone else involved."

"What are you suggesting?"

"Please sit down old chap. Looking up at people always makes me feel tired."

Leo settled himself on the edge of the couch and stared resolutely at the floor, fiddling with his finger nails, waiting for him to continue.

"Soul mates don't always find each other in every life time," said Jonesy. "It's sad of course, but in the overall scheme of things, a life time is no more than the blink of an eye." He paused and waited for a reaction. "Do you understand what I'm talking about?"

Leo nodded, eyes still fixed on the floor.

"Caroline Blanchard has gone to quite extraordinary lengths to make contact with you. But there's something missing here." Jonesy reached for his notes. "You haven't told me what your wife thought about moving to 'Pelham Green Farm House'."

"At first she didn't like the idea at all," said Leo. "Old house, too far from London, that sort of thing. Then, I think it was after the second visit, she seemed to change her mind and became quite enthusiastic. But she's never liked the 1930's extension."

"Would you say you were happily married at that time?"

"I thought so. Yes."

"And now?"

"Now there's Caroline, everything's changed and Angela wants a divorce."

"Is there another man?" Jonesy hesitated. "I'm sorry to barge into your private life like this but it's important."

Leo leaned back against the arm of the couch. "Angela's been seeing Tim Thatcher, the chap who owns the estate agency," he whispered.

"How long has it been going on?"

"No idea."

"I wonder," said Jonesy, popping another mint into his mouth, "if Mr Thatcher might be the 'someone else' I have in mind." He smiled to himself. "Perhaps I'll pay him a visit one day very soon."

"Visit Tim? Why?"

"Because he's the common factor." Jonesy slapped his notes down on the couch. "First he sent you Caroline Blanchard's house and then he sent you Caroline Blanchard while your wife, who wasn't keen on the house to begin with, seems to have quickly warmed to both the house and the man. Take away the Tim Thatcher factor and you'd probably still be happily living in Chelsea with your wife."

"What exactly are you getting at?"

"Sorry but what I do is never 'exactly' anything and I'm not sure what I'm *'getting at'* yet myself. Things should be clearer in a couple of days."

Leo glanced across at the man sprawled out at the other end of the couch. "I've been meaning to ask," he said. "What do you do?"

"Much the same as Tim Thatcher I suppose," said Jonesy. "He provides a professional link between buyers and sellers; I make more tortuous links between the living and the dead."

"A medium then?"

Jonesy shook his head. "No labels please. It's a perfectly natural process." He plumped up his cushions and carefully rearranged them, points upwards, in the corner of the couch before he stood up and made towards the door, bringing the meeting to an abrupt close. "One last thing before you go," he said. "Best if you didn't mention me to Caroline Blanchard. Not yet anyway."

"Caroline?" Leo looked surprised. "You think she'll contact me again?"

"Definitely," said Jonesy. "You can rely on it."

Chapter Seven

A thick roll of newspapers, wedged tight in the letter box, reminded Angela Gannesh that it was Sunday, the worst day of the week. Not this morning the comforting weekday hum of distant rush hour traffic, reassuring proof of human life beyond the front gates, instead the solemn toll of church bells and a pious, joyless gloom, smothering the morning like a wet blanket.

Paddy, still dozing on the upstairs landing, stretched out, waiting for Leo to open his bedroom door, slapped a listless tail on the carpet in recognition as she passed on her way down to the kitchen, a flouncy cotton beach wrap hanging loose from her shoulders, stiletto heel slippers clackety clicking on the wooden stairs.

She sat in silence by the pool, a cup of coffee on the teak table by her side, flicking through the colour magazine; pretentious models in preposterous clothes and then, in black and white, the pale, flimsy pages of the real world, dismal headlines to dull a warm, sunny morning.

Angela draped the beach wrap across the back of a chair, carefully adjusted thin gold straps on a black satin bikini and settled herself on the sun lounger, head back resting on a rolled-up towel, trying not to think about Tim's behaviour the night before.

Grilled chops on a cold plate, greasy and unappetising with a limp, wet salad, didn't live up to Tim's earlier promise of a romantic candle-lit dinner for two. Nothing romantic about a pork chop but at least he'd tried. What upset her was the absurd invitation to move-in with him, live together in that pokey little flat. Ridiculous. A few tiny rooms above a high street shop might, in the wonky world of estate agents, be a desirable bijou apartment, intimate, unpretentious, with considerable scope for improvement, but Angela didn't see it that way. To her it was

124

just one small room away from a bed-sit and she told him so. Which is when things started to go wrong.

Tim's words echoed in her head. Perhaps he was right but she made no apologies for wanting to live in a prestigious house, drive a quality car, and enjoy a comfortable life-style. And she wasn't going to be called a spoilt, money-grabbing, stuck-up bitch by anyone, especially someone who'd obviously had too much to drink. She'd slammed the door behind her when she left so the sound of shattering glass could have been the ornate fluted pane in the top panel. No point in looking back to find out and, anyway, it was more likely to be one of Tim's empty bottles of Mouton Cadet, flung down the stairs in childish rage.

"Mind if I join you?" Leo's voice from the upstairs window. "I'll bring some more coffee."

She waved a newspaper in reply, not bothering to turn round, slipped blue tinted sunglasses over tired eyes and stared up at a cloudless summer sky. A constant stream of high street traffic, viewed from the first floor window of a pokey little flat was no match for the cool tranquillity of a country garden. No way.

"I brought you another cup," said Leo sitting down opposite. "Shall I?" He held the coffee pot aloft for a moment.

"Please, yes." She sat up, slipped her glasses further down her nose, and peered over the top. "You're growing a moustache," she said quietly. "Suits you."

Leo smoothed his upper lip with thumb and forefinger. "Everyone's growing them. That film 'Viva Zapata' or something."

Angela sat, motionless, studying his face. "Makes you look years younger," she said. "All you need now are the flared trousers and kipper tie."

"Hold it right there," he said emphatically. "I've made my concession to seventies fashion. Let's not go mad."

A lone pigeon waddled importantly across the lawn, head held high, plump breast puffed out like a huge double chin; then a sudden and undignified dash for the safety of the trees, flapping and fluttering, followed by a gangling dog.

Leo poured the coffee carefully into two cups and placed one on the table next to Angela "Who's going to have custody of Paddy," he said.

"I hadn't thought about it." Angela lifted her sunglasses and stared across the lawn. "Besides, he's your dog."

"He's our dog."

"OK he's our dog," she snapped. "I'll have him every other weekend and for a week in the school holidays. We'll draw lots for Christmas. Will that do?"

Leo decided the question didn't deserve an answer. He leaned back in the chair, hands limply at his side, legs out straight in front of him, and pursed his lips into an impotent whistle. Paddy bounded over from beyond the silver birch trees.

"We've got something to tell you old chap," he said, running his fingers through the long grey fur. "Your mother and I are getting a divorce.".

Angela turned away quickly, looking back towards the house. "Stop it Leo. It's not funny."

"No it's not funny, is it?" Leo paused for a moment, sipped his coffee. "But then I never expected a divorce to be funny. How could it be?"

She slipped the towel back behind her head and rearranged herself on the sun lounger: "Then we won't have one," she said abruptly. "Let's just forget all about it, carry on as before."

Leo was taken by surprise. "Are you sure that's what you want?"

"Quite sure. Why don't you move back into the bedroom? Today if you like."

He raised himself slowly out of the chair, mild perspiration glistening on his head, and walked away from her towards the edge of the pool. He stood for a while looking down at the cool mirror surface of the water. "And what about what I want?" he said quietly.

She pushed her sunglasses up into her hair, a hard-won smile on her face. "Come on now darling, let's stop this." She held out her hand. "The Tim Thatcher thing is over, finished, I promise."

He turned to face her. "Is that all it was, just a 'thing'?"

"That's all it ever was, just a silly and stupid thing. Nothing more. I'm sorry for what happened, really I am." She looked up at him coyly, stroked her hair gently away from her eyes. "Please forgive me darling," she whispered.

Leo thrust his hands deep into his pockets and glanced up at the faint white shadow of the moon lingering in the morning sky. "Suppose I had a 'thing' with someone. Would you forgive me?"

She stared for a while into her coffee cup before answering. "But you wouldn't, would you?" she said eventually. "You're not the type."

"I expect you're right." He positioned a large green and white umbrella behind his chair and sat down facing the pool. "All the same, how would you feel about it if I did?"

"I'd wonder why."

"Suppose I said I'd fallen in love."

"But you wouldn't have the time to fall in love with someone else."

"Why not? Some of the most beautiful girls in London come through my office every day. It would be easy."

Angela fanned herself with the colour magazine. "You said love Leo. Those little trollops would only want you for your money."

"OK, let's assume you're right and I was having a 'thing' with a golddigging trollop. How would you feel about it?"

127

"I'd feel terribly sorry for you."

Leo stared out across the pool. "Do you know I hadn't expected pity? Jealousy, or anger perhaps, possibly even a slight tinge of broken heart. But not pity."

"Don't worry, after the pity would come the rage," she said coolly. "Along with the divorce."

"No second chance for me then?"

"Face facts Leo. If some little gold digger ever got her claws into you I'd have to protect myself."

"But just suppose this woman wasn't interested in my money or worldly possessions. Let's say she didn't want anything. "

"In your dreams Leo my love."

He nodded. "Very probably Angela, very probably."

She twisted her hair into an elastic band and made towards the far end of the pool where she sat down, kicking her feet about in the water, head back, the sun shining on her face. "Your hypothetical woman, the one who isn't interested in your money," she shouted. "Does she exist?"

"Not really, no."

"Thought not." She slipped gently into the water and floated on her back towards the centre of the pool.

Leo closed his eyes to the sun's glare and settled back in the chair, shoes off, legs crossed, hands in his lap, relaxed. The rhythmic slap of water against the edges of the pool, somewhere behind him a pigeon cooing, a warm summer breeze whispering softly across his face.

"In your dreams." Angela's words, now faint and fading, but still ringing in his ears and then the giddy scent of Caroline Blanchard suddenly around him, embracing, comforting. "They're our dreams Leo," she said softly. "Our once upon a time."

The hazy outline of the summer house to his right, wooden tables and chairs arranged outside and, at the edge of the lawn, the bronze statue of a woman dancing. Caroline, sitting opposite, perfectly still, smiling, her hands outstretched across the table, reaching for his.

Leo tried to speak but surrendered to an easy, natural silence. There was nothing to be said, no painful words, no searching questions; why she was there, what she wanted. No need to say anything.   She would already know why he couldn't start a new life with her - not yet, not now.

The tips of her fingers caressed his brow, gently closed his eyes and touched his lips for a fleeting moment. Then silence. Everything still.

A spray of water, cold and smelling of chlorine, shocked the senses. Leo lurched back, quickly wiped his face with his hand, eyes wide open to two splashing feet immediately below him and Angela's screams.

"Why don't you come in? Can't just sit there baking in the sun. You'll burn."

He brushed the damp from his shirt as he stood up. "Not really in the mood right now," he said. "Perhaps later." He started towards the house, promising himself to give some serious thought to the idea of dying.

Justin Charlton-Jones had made it all seem very simple. If that brandy had been poison and if he'd swigged it down it would all be over and done with by now. Paradise – maybe.

The bar was cool, on the opposite of the house to the midday sun. A drink seemed like a good idea. He took two wine glasses from the shelf without thinking and placed them on the top of the bar with a bottle of chilled Chablis from the small fridge below. Jonesy's Belgravia telephone number, lots of two's and three's, easy to remember, quickly dialled with one hand while the other poured the wine. Six rings before he answered. Sunday lunch time, of course, not a good time to call.

"Charlton-Jones." The voice was clipped.

Leo cleared his throat. "Leo Gannesh here. Sorry to interrupt your Sunday." He paused to sip his wine. "I just wondered if you'd talked to Tim Thatcher yet."

"Yesterday. I visited him."

"Oh, right. Thank you. That was quick."

"I thought it was best."

Leo hesitated, unsure exactly what to say next. "Did you find out anything?"

"Quite a lot actually. It's a very unusual business."

"How do you mean?"

"Look, I wonder if we could talk about this tomorrow sometime?"

"So sorry. Yes of course. What's a good time to ring you?"

"Not on the `phone. I was planning to come down to see you - and the house. Say eleven?"

"Fine. Look forward to seeing you."

It occurred to Leo that he had no idea how much of a bill Jonesy might be running up on his behalf. Anyway, too late now. He set the two glasses and the bottle on a silver tray, slid the bar stool to one side with his foot, and set off back to the pool.

Angela, wet bikini top hanging loosely from the umbrella pole, slapped her thigh to a tuneless, muddled sound from a tinny transistor radio which rattled into earshot like nails in a jar. She held out her hand in anticipation while Leo poured the wine.

"What shall we drink to?" she said quietly as he passed her the ice cold drink.

Leo raised his glass. "To the good times."

"The good times," she repeated. "And lots more of them."

He settled himself under the umbrella, slipped off his shoes, and loosened the sleeves of his shirt. "Not so sure it's a good idea to bare your boobs to the midday sun," he said.

"Don't be silly. Topless tans are in fashion." She smiled, ran

130

her fingers lightly across her breasts then spread her arms wide. "My extremities won't be so white and spiteful after a few days in the sun Leo. Promise."

"Perhaps you could forget tomorrow morning if you wouldn't mind. I've got a chap coming over for a meeting."

"Don't worry," she said covering herself coyly with a towel. "I won't embarrass you."

At eleven o'clock precisely Justin Charlton-Jones unfolded himself wearily from the driving seat of a white Mini Cooper and stretched to his full height, hands reaching up, fingers grabbing at the sky. He took a small brown leather suitcase from the boot of the car and strode purposefully over to the front porch where he stood, unmoving, for nearly fifteen minutes before he finally rang the doorbell.

Leo had barely opened the front door before Paddy pushed his way out into the drive, circled the white car twice, and followed the two men into the lounge, tail wagging.

"This is a positive room," said Jonesy. "Lots of happiness here." He stared up at the ceiling. "The problem, I think, may be up there, the room above us." He placed the suitcase to one side of the couch.

Paddy led the way upstairs and into the green bedroom.

"Sorry it's a bit of a mess." Leo hurriedly straightened the duvet as best he could. "Got up a bit later than planned." He picked up some socks from beside the bed and tossed them, with a crumpled shirt, into a green wicker basket in the corner of the room.

Jonesy stood in front of the window, looking out over the garden. "Please don't tidy up for me," he murmured. "I want to see the room as it was then, twenty five years ago; her room." He turned round and walked slowly past Leo, back to the door. "This is where she ended it," he said after a long pause. "A winter's evening - snowy, still, and very cold. The bed - over there." He pointed across the room towards the chest of drawers. "And an oil painting, a woman with yellow flowers, buttercups perhaps, on the wall opposite. Dresses, lots of them, scattered around the room. Unsure what to wear - wants to look her best when they find her."

Leo was uneasy. "Can I get you a coffee?" he said. "In the garden, perhaps."

Jonesy shook his head and sat down on the edge of the bed. "Music special music." He leaned back on his elbows, eyes closed, listening, hearing something in the silence. "She plays it over and over again," he whispered. "Her mother's favourite record, `September in the rain'. The long dress, silky white, the one she's chosen, her mother's dress."

"I think that's enough," Leo said abruptly. He opened wide the bedroom door and stood beside it holding the handle.

Jonesy sat up, slowly twisted himself round towards the voice and Leo's sullen frown. "I'm not completely sure why she did it," he said, rubbing his eyes. "But Champagne and sleeping pills took away the terrible guilt she felt about someone else, someone close."

"Does it matter how and why?"

"It matters to Caroline Blanchard . She knows now what should have been, would have been, if she could have waited and tried to face up to whatever it was she'd done." Jonesy stood up. "She's not alone. There are others like her waiting for their special people to join them."

Leo shrugged. "Ghosts you mean?"

"I prefer earth-bound spirits," said Jonesy. "Much less theatrical. This is not about spooks, chain rattling and things that go bump in the night." He walked over to the door and stood in front of Leo. "This is a soul with deep regrets and there, but for the grace of God......"

They walked downstairs together in silence then back to the lounge where Leo quickly plumped up the cushions on the couch and invited his guest to sit down. "I'm glad you think this is a positive room," he said. "It's where I last saw Caroline."

Jonesy stared into the mirrored mosaic fireplace and smiled. "Do you think we could have that coffee now? I've got a lot to tell you."

"How do you like your coffee Mr .....umm I'm sorry, we haven't been introduced." Angela standing demurely in the doorway, a Chinese shantung dress, turquoise and black, hugging her body, hair twisted into a chic pleat at the back. She crossed the room, hand extended, a modest smile on glossy pale pink lips. "I'm Angela, Leo's wife. Please don't get up."

Leo shifted in his chair. "This is Mr Charlton-Jones," he said blandly without further explanation.

"Let me guess." Angela stood in front of the couch, her finger gently tracing the line of her lips. "You're a photographer."

"Nothing so exotic I'm afraid." Jonesy leaned forward and looked up at her. "But you must surely be a model."

"Used to be. Not anymore." She started back towards the door then turned, eyes wide and expectant. "Are you in the fashion business Mr Charlton-Jones?"

"Communications," he said quietly. "And please call me Jonesy."

Angela stood stock-still in the doorway. "And how do you take your coffee Jonesy?"

"Strong, black, and no sugar."

She nodded, smoothed her dress over her hips with both hands and went off to the kitchen.

"I assume Angela doesn't know why I'm here," said Jonesy, sliding himself back into the comfort of the couch.

"She knows nothing about all this." Leo thought for a moment. "Perhaps we should have coffee in the garden."

Jonesy's eyes flickered. "Who's Helen?" he said suddenly.

"Angela's mother."

"No problem then. Your wife's meeting her for lunch."

133

"Unlikely, it's Monday," said Leo. "She has lunch with her mother on Thursdays."

Jonesy slowly shook his head. "I'm afraid she usually has sex with Mr Thatcher on Thursdays."

The conversation faltered as Angela appeared with a tray, placed it carefully on top of the fireplace, and poured two cups of coffee. "Sorry, we haven't got around to sorting out side tables in here yet," she said, handing a cup to Jonesy. "We've been a bit unsure about the decor, haven't we darling?"

Leo ignored the jibe. "Not joining us?" he said, taking a cup from the tray.

"Sorry, things to do, then a quick bite of lunch with Ma." She blew Leo a kiss. "Biscuits if you want them," she said then quickly left the room.

Jonesy waited for the footsteps to fade. "I think she probably heard me," he whispered.

"Good," said Leo wearily. "I always thought there were far too many Thursday's in Angela's week."

There were two loud blasts on her car horn as she crossed in front of the house then the sound of spinning tyres grinding into the shingle along the drive and down to the front gates.

Jonesy took a biscuit, snapped it neatly into four pieces and dunked them, each in turn, in his coffee. "Caroline Blanchard returns to this room quite often," he announced. "It was where she was most happy and contented - this and the garden."

"I like the room too," said Leo. "There's something about it."

"The `*something about it'* is Caroline Blanchard, or at least the fading impressions of her life which linger here." He stood up, placed his cup back on the tray and moved slowly around the room, head tilted to one side then the other, listening, breathing deeply. "She wanted you here in this house, to be near you."

Leo fidgeted uncomfortably in his chair. "Caroline was

134

rather more than a fading impression when I first met her - when we all met her at the dinner party. Flesh and blood, talking, laughing, eating and drinking." He waited while Jonesy messed about, irritatingly, with the top of the percolator before pouring himself another coffee. "How did she do it?" he asked when he was sure Jonesy had quite finished fiddling.

"With help from Tim Thatcher." Jonesy's voice had a new resonance, the words suddenly more rounded and concise. "What you all experienced was an illusion which the two of them carefully created for your benefit. They presented you with the image you were expecting, perhaps wanted to see, a young woman called Caroline Blanchard."

"What does that make Tim Thatcher, some kind of illusionist?"

"I'd say he was an accomplice, a collaborator, someone with the ability to reinforce the presence of a whimsical spirit to make it seem completely real."

Leo thought for a moment slowly shaking his head. "No," he mumbled quietly. "No, that doesn't explain the other times."

"What other times?" said Jonesy.

"The two meetings I had alone with Caroline. Tim Thatcher couldn't possibly have reinforced anything - he wasn't there."

Jonesy, chin resting on a clenched fist, stared down at his long black boots. "On both occasions you picked-up Caroline Blanchard from Thatcher's," he said. "I'll wager he was there each time."

"Yes he was, but only for a matter of minutes."

"Sufficient to reinforce the image, set the scene so to speak. Then it was up to Caroline to prolong the illusion." Jonesy looked across to the fire place. "Like a short film, Tim the director, Caroline the star, eventually it had to end. But I'm fairly sure Caroline has some more personal appearances lined up for you, here in the house."

"No more collaboration from Tim Thatcher then?"

"No, his job's done. He brought you to this house, introduced you to Caroline Blanchard and, dare I say it, entertained your wife while he was about it." Jonesy glanced at his watch. "Can I buy you a drink?" he said.

Leo pulled himself out of the chair, hoisted his trousers with both hands and started towards the door. "We could have one here if you like."

"Thanks," said Jonesy. "But if it's all the same with you, I was rather hoping we could pay a short visit to Paula Maxwell's pub. Never been there - not even sure what it's called?"

"The Kings Oak'. Why not? Good idea." He stopped abruptly, hand gently rubbing his forehead. "On the phone you mentioned that you'd been to see Tim Thatcher."

"That's right. Gave him my details as someone looking for an old character house in the area."

"And are you?"

"Not me, I'm a city dweller." He reached for the suitcase, clicked it open as he placed it on his lap and took out some property details with the green and black 'Thatchers' logo on the top. "I needed a reason to observe Tim Thatcher at first hand, test my hypotheses."

Leo nodded solemnly and tried to appear suitably impressed. He collected his keys from the hall table and led the way out and across the drive to the black Rolls Royce, parked at the side of the house. "What exactly were you hypothesising about?"

"An alternative agenda, a second element in the estate agency business." Jonesy ran his hand casually across the polished walnut dashboard. "The chap who owned this car before you," he said quietly. "Was he an actor or comedian, something like that? Quite well known anyway?"

"Actor. He was in that TV series about some kind of secret service department. Good actor, rotten script." Leo glanced down at the property details laying on the seat between them. "But please go on with your hypotheses. I'm intrigued."

Jonesy flipped through the papers and slid the details of two properties across the seat. "These two houses have been on the market for more than four months. Both houses are well presented, reasonably priced and in good locations but there have been no offers on either."

"There's probably a sewage farm down the road or a railway line running through the back garden."

"No," Jonesy said emphatically. "I've visited both and couldn't fault either. That's not why they are still on the market."

"So what's the problem?"

"That's my hypotheses, the alternative agenda." Jonesy snuggled back in the seat and gazed out at the traffic dawdling towards the town. "Tim Thatcher goes to considerable trouble to find very special buyers for some of his houses; people who'll pay the asking price to the current owner - but only after they've been selected by a previous owner."

Leo frowned. "Sorry, you've lost me. What's it got to do with a previous owner."

"Everything if the previous owner's still in residence, like Caroline Blanchard at 'Pelham Green Farm House' for example."

"Oh come on now. How often does that happen?"

"Perhaps more often than you might think," said Jonesy. "Tim Thatcher seems to find buyers who are compatible with, shall we say, the spirit of the house."

"You mean he gets on with the ghosts?"

"I'm coming to that bit." Jonesy patted the top of the dashboard. "Most people wouldn't notice the atmosphere in an old car but they would probably sense something in an old house. They might say it had a nice feeling when, in fact, they were picking up the vibrations of its past."

137

Leo stopped the car outside the pub then quickly reversed back up the road to the shade of a sycamore tree and switched off the engine. "The problem with your hypotheses is that most of the spirits in Tim Thatcher's world are the liquid kind," he said with a throaty chuckle. "But psychic powers? I don't think so."

"That's the odd thing about it." Jonesy stared at him with dark brown eyes. "Neither do I"

"Surely that rather shoots down your hypotheses?" said Leo.

"Not if he's an accomplice and the power rests with Caroline Blanchard." Jonesy hesitated for a moment before he continued. "Not if there is a bond between them."

Leo slammed the car door behind him and stalked off towards The Kings Oak'. "You know I don't really think I like your hypotheses," he shouted.

"That's rather irrelevant if I may say so." Jonesy tugged at the top of his boots, wiggled his feet about for a moment then slowly turned around, hands on hips, taking in the surrounding countryside."

"Are you coming?" Leo yelled as he reached the open doors of the pub.

Jonesy stopped and rested an elbow on the chrome radiator grill, raised the other arm in a limp, summoning wave and waited in silence.

"What is it?" Leo huffed part way back to the car.

"An hypotheses," said Jonesy with clipped syllables, eyes firmly focussed on a small patch of grass in front of him, "is a supposition intended to explain a set of circumstances, based on the evidence which may be available." He slowly raised his head until their eyes met. "And, to be perfectly honest, I don't care tuppence whether you like it or not."

But you were suggesting that Caroline and Tim............."

Jonesy interrupted. "I was suggesting only that there was a bond between them. You decided the rest for yourself." He

138

dabbed his brow with a red silk handkerchief and loosened his shirt cuffs "Now, if you would care to walk with me at a less petulant pace, I should be pleased to join you for lunch."

Leo nodded. "Sorry. Didn't mean to offend."

Paula Maxwell, ill-advised maroon silk kaftan billowing in the afternoon breeze, appeared at the door, one arm raised in greeting, a torchless Statue of Liberty on the pub steps. "Thought it was you Leo," she called. "Not leaving already are you?"

"Brought someone to see you."

Jonesy walked ahead, hands reaching out. "How long has it been?"

"Too long," she said wistfully, wrapping her arms around him. "Much too long."

Leo stood back and waited until the spontaneous display of affection had subsided before following them into the bar, hands behind his back like a distant relative at a wedding. "You've obviously known each other a long time," he said after they'd settled themselves at an oblong table in the bay window of the restaurant, the two men on one side, Paula on the other, the apex of a triangle.

"Must be five years." Jonesy grabbed Paula's hand reassuringly as if the memory might arouse sensitive emotions. "1966 it was, the year we won the World Cup."

"Funny, I didn't have you pegged as a football fan," said Leo.

"I'm not. Hate the game, but you couldn't get away from it that July. Seemed like the whole country had gone barmy."

Paula raised what was left of the gin and tonic she'd picked up on her way through the bar and spoke in a theatrical voice. "To the man who saved my life," she announced to the rest of the restaurant. "Without his extraordinary powers I'd probably be dead." She emptied the glass, placed it ceremoniously in the centre of the table and gave Jonesy a reverent smile. "We've stayed in touch ever since."

Leo, eye brows raised in expectation, stared at each of them in turn, waiting for the rest of the story to unfold. "I suppose someone is going to explain what happened?" he said after a long pause.

"Honestly, it was nothing," said Jonesy. "Giles and Paula were getting into their car after a dinner party. We'd barely spoken to each other during the evening but I suddenly felt that they shouldn't go. I went outside and asked them if they'd mind waiting for half an hour."

"And thank goodness we did." Paula slammed her hand down firmly on the table. "If we'd left any earlier our car would have been slap bang in the middle of a multiple pile up on the motorway." She shook her head, eyes tightly shut, shuddering at the prospect.

"Amazing," said Leo looking around for the waitress. "That's really quite incredible." He left a decent interval, nodding quietly, before he changed the subject. "Do you think Tim Thatcher will be in this lunch time?"

"Unlikely," she said. "Monday's usually his busy day, after all the weekend activity. He'll probably drop in this evening."

"Do you think Tim would mind if Jonesy here borrowed his chair during lunch?"

Paula lit a cigarette and drew her breath in sharply. "It's not Tim's chair," she snapped indignantly, blowing smoke high into the air. "He may monopolise it but he doesn't own it." She stopped short, realizing her voice had jumped an octave. "Anyway, why do you want it?" she asked in a more moderated tone.

"I'd like to know a little more about him," said Jonesy. "Thought the chair might open up some doors so to speak."

Paula stared back quizzically, tapping the ash from the end of her cigarette with a tobacco stained finger. "I think that's as much as I want to know," she said. "I'll get the chair sent in."

140

She picked up her glass and went back to the bar, returning almost at once with two hand written menu cards and some insider information on the Dover sole; a bit on the small side.

A restaurant chair, faded tapestry upholstery and an uncompromising knobbly back, was happily exchanged for the mellow curves of Tim's favourite Windsor, complete with velvet cushion. Jonesy sat down cautiously and rubbed his hands across the shiny smooth wood.

"Will you be able to eat *and* concentrate on whatever it is you're doing with Tim's chair?" said Leo touching his forehead with two fingers as if he might be expecting a telepathic message.

Jonesy leaned back and closed his eyes. "No concentration necessary, you simply have to let the feelings flow."

"And are they - flowing I mean?"

"Not exactly, but I'm sure they will."

Two Dover soles, small but well presented, were delivered to the table with a selection of vegetables in a large, green cabbage leaf dish and a decanter of house white wine.

Paula, clutching a large gin and tonic and an empty ashtray, hovered to one side while the waitress fluttered around the table, spreading starched white linen across laps with the proficiency of a hospital nurse, asking if everything was *'OK for you'* for the umpteenth time, before marching her trolley back to the kitchen.

"Do you mind if I smoke while you eat?" Paula sat down, took a pink cigarette from a box of king-size cork tips with gold bands around the end and wished them both `bon appetit'. She lit the cigarette without waiting for an answer.

Leo wasn't good at silence, it made him feel uneasy, especially during a meal. He was grateful for the clatter of cutlery when the waitress eventually cleared things away, wiped bread crumbs into a cupped hand with a crumpled napkin and generally tidied-up the table.

"Was everything OK for you?" she asked again, placing a spoon and fork in front of each of them. "We've got apple pie with either custard or cream, a sherry trifle and one crème caramel."

"Nothing for me thanks," said Jonesy staring thoughtfully into middle distance.

Leo gently patting his belly and shook his head. "Just a coffee," he said. "Black, no sugar."

The Windsor chair squealed across the slate tiled floor as Jonesy eased himself back from the table.

"I think Tim Thatcher's the reason Caroline Blanchard killed herself," he said wearily. "All that guilt, too many regrets." He stood up slowly and slid the chair to one side, then drew up another and slumped down heavily like a boxer in his corner at the end of a punishing round. "She was very young, early twenties perhaps."

Paula grasped Leo's hand before he could interrupt.

Jonesy hesitated for a moment, rubbing his brow, trying hard to picture something, something important. He looked again at the chair, gently touched the arm.

"Caroline was his mother," he whispered. "Tim was sent away for adoption soon after he was born. Not Caroline's idea, her father's. She wasn't really given much of a choice."

Leo gazed blankly at the cup of coffee which had just been placed in front of him and permitted himself a moment of quiet to rake through Jonesy's words. "It's no bloody wonder he drinks so much," he muttered to himself.

Paula shrugged her shoulders, adjusted her top and slipped quietly away from the table with a deep sigh.

"Lunch was on the house," she called back as she started towards the bar.

Jonesy nonchalantly flicked his finger nail against the rim of an empty wine glass. It rang out five or six times, like the chimes of a church clock, before he spoke. "What are you going to do about Caroline Blanchard?" he asked. "You can't allow this situation to continue."

Leo thought for a second, pushed his cup and saucer to one side and leaned forward, hands flat on the table. "What can I do? I don't want to live without her but I certainly don't want to die to be with her."

"Dying, living? They're one and the same," said Jonesy, giving the wine glass a final ping before standing up. "I'm afraid they're inseparable, indistinguishable and utterly inevitable. All over in the blink of an eye."

"Is that supposed to be an answer?" Leo dug deep into his pockets and found a handful of small change which he left beside the coffee cup.

"Take control." Jonesy's words, clipped and concise, sounded like a warning. "Do it as soon as possible," he said. "It's important."

"How?" Leo, beads of perspiration on his brow, stood motionless. "How do I take control?"

"Tell her the truth," said Jonesy. "Tell her you love her then tell her to go, to leave you alone for what's left of your natural life. But ask her, also, to wait for you and a new time together."

"That makes sense." Leo dabbed his forehead with a handkerchief. "I'm sure that's the right thing to do."

"I'm not," Jonesy replied. "I'm not sure at all."

"What the hell does that mean?"

Jonesy's supreme self-confidence seemed to evaporate, his face more pale. "It means," he whispered, almost as an apology, "that I've never dealt with anything quite like this before. To be perfectly frank, I'm not sure."

Leo ran a finger around the inside of his shirt collar as he struggled to fix the knot in his tie then carefully buttoned-up the front of his jacket and stepped away from the table. "Thanks anyway Jonesy," he said with a weak but genuine smile. "Thanks for everything."

Chapter Eight

Not walking under ladders wasn't so much a superstition as plain common sense. Even if the devil didn't manage to make off with your soul, or whatever he was supposed to do if you passed through the triangle formed by the ladder and the wall, there remained the distinct possibility of a pot of paint, or worse, falling on your head. So Leo Gannesh didn't do it.

On Friday morning, when the decorators started rubbing down the paintwork on the outside of 'Pelham Green Farm House', there were two extension ladders leaning at forty five degrees against the eaves. The one directly over the front door presented the clear and unavoidable risk of Satan's wrath to anyone daring to venture in or out of the house. And it was the thirteenth day of the month. A folded 'Times' newspaper held protectively over his head, brief case under his arm, Leo stepped warily around a crouched figure with a blowtorch and made a dash for the garage block.

Twenty minutes later, on the outer fringes of London, where Surrey's leafy green lanes wilted and withered into grey streets of concrete, more suicidal office workers than usual stepped out from their kerbside huddles and into the path of the black Rolls Royce. Unseeing, uncaring, people with a sub-conscious death wish, like the chap sauntering across the road with the overweight corgi, deaf to the chorus of horns, blind to the danger.

It was different in Bond Street where pedestrian-power ruled and groups of individuals regularly swarmed across the road as one, bringing the traffic to a sudden halt on a collective whim. Leo waited patiently before turning left into Conduit Street and reversing into his usual space at the Westbury Hotel, quarter of an hour late for the ten o'clock opening of 'Birds' boutique which, with any luck, would be over and done with by the time he arrived. He'd look in as promised, offer his congratulations, politely decline a glass of tepid white wine and make a hasty exit after some superficial chit chat with Sammy Silverman's bank manager, landlord, shopfitter, neighbours, close friends, relatives and all the other guests. But that's not how it went.

Traffic in Kingley Street was at a complete standstill when Leo's taxi dropped him outside a run down cafe and quickly reversed back up the road, leaving him to grapple with the crowds gathered outside 'Birds' boutique. Half a dozen press photographers yelled instructions from their vantage point in the gutter to a young girl wearing a long blue wig and little else, who posed uneasily in the shop window.

"Flick yer `air back. Stick yer bum out. Mouth open wider, big smile. Bend yer knees a bit. Give us a pout." Directions to challenge the most accomplished contortionist, which failed to penetrate the thick plate glass window and were quickly drowned by the music blasting out from a large speaker just inside the door. 'The Byrds', an American group with a hit record from the sixties, *'Mr Tambourine Man'*.

Sammy Silverman, an oversized yellow bow tie clinging to his neck like a jaundiced bat, shouted encouragement to the back of the blue wig from the relative safety of the shirt counter. "Flap your arms," he called out. "Remember you're a blue tit."

Four girls in feather-trimmed bikinis, largely ignored as they dangled precariously from the ceiling on swings, twisted and turned above the clothes rails, smiling nervously, trying their best to resemble canaries.

Outside the shop the press pack had given-up on Sammy Silverman's blue tit. Cameras stopped flashing and hung heavily around weary necks while one of them went inside to sort out the problem.

"We need her boobs in the picture," he shouted across the shop to the shirt counter. "A 'blue tit' not Modesty Blaise."

Leo fought his way through the gawpers, wedged tight and unmoving in the narrow doorway, and struggled across the shop over to the window. "We don't do topless," he said quietly, helping the blue tit down from her perch. "Go and put your clothes on."

"Hold on just a moment." Sammy Silverman adjusted the yellow bat at his throat and made towards the window. "We need her for the picture. "Blue tits," he said, cupping his hands in front of his chest in case Leo hadn't quite grasped the analogy.

"If you wanted whores you should have gone to a brothel," Leo snapped. "And you can, get yourselves down from there too," he shouted up to the four canaries. "Get dressed and go."

Sammy Silverman waved a plump finger under Leo's nose. "It's breach of contract. I'll sue."

"It's pornography and you can do what you like," said Leo, turning away to leave.

The suitably dramatic exit, quickly halted by a sudden surge of people around the two men, set cameras flashing above the heads of the crowd as photographers jostled for a ringside position on top of the shirt counter.

"Stick one on 'im Sam," someone yelled from the back of the shop. "Kick 'im art."

Leo stood stock-still for a moment then turned slowly back and looked daggers at the dumpy figure standing in front of him. "Yes, why don't you do that Sammy - in full view of all these press photographers? That should get you some cheap publicity."

"I'll sue," Silverman repeated angrily as Leo pushed a path back towards the door and out into the street where two police officers had started to break-up the crowd, sending them on their way with random warnings about causing an obstruction.

At the bottom of Kingley Street, where Beak Street showed the way out of the narrow Soho lanes and into the relative

146

charm of Regent Street, Leo paused to look back up the road, now almost deserted except for a police car waiting, lights still flashing, outside 'Birds' boutique. A fickle crowd had dispersed in seconds, like quicksilver, streaming swiftly back into the safe, shallow nooks and crannies of normal life. Gone without trace for the moment but back tomorrow, maybe, if blue tits and canaries earned a place in the morning papers.

The taxi cab acknowledged Leo's wave with a quick flash of its headlights, made an anti-social U-turn in the middle of the road and came to an abrupt halt in front of the post box. "Where to Guv, Buckingham Palace or Big Ben?"

"Bond Street. Bottom end." Leo settled himself in the back as the cab swung into Regent Street, then leaned forward and slid the small glass communications window to one side. "Do I look like a tourist?" he asked politely.

"No mate. But they always want to go to the Palace after Carnaby Street, that or Parliament Square."

"After Carnaby Street?" Leo queried.

"Yes mate. Carnaby Street's top of the list for most of 'em, especially the yanks. Taken over from the Tower it has."

Leo gently closed the window and slumped back into the seat. What, he wondered, had the world come to when a row of tatty boutiques could threaten the Tower of London as the top tourist attraction. He thought back to his first visit as a child; Traitors Gate, the Bloody Tower, but there were no traitors and definitely no blood, not even the suggestion of a stain. Disappointing for a child. More chance of blood and treachery at 'Birds' boutique.

By the time the cab drew up, on the wrong side of the road, opposite the office, Leo's pulse rate had returned to normal and he was ready for anything the rest of Friday the thirteenth might throw at him, anything, that is, except Lucy. Leo didn't like cats, particularly Siamese cats and especially cats like Lucy who sharpened their claws on delicate rubber plants and

147

piddled in inaccessible places.

Lucy glared menacingly from an improvised bed of magazines and newspapers spread haphazardly across a low, coffee table in the corner of the reception. She rose slowly to her feet as Leo passed, thin, boney legs rigid and perfectly straight, back arched, fur bristling, mouth stretched into a spine-chilling whine - a warning, a challenge, an insult, possibly all three.

"I don't think your cat likes me," Leo called out. "She seems slightly on edge."

Claudia Hamilton's head appeared around the door. "It's nothing personal, she just doesn't like men."

"Well I'd hate to antagonize her. How long will she be staying?"

"Just for the week, as I said, while there's nobody in the flat."

"Do you think the rubber plant will last that long?"

Claudia sucked air through her teeth. "Sorry about that."

She followed Leo into his office. "How was 'Birds' boutique?" she asked, slipping into her usual chair, note book in hand.

Leo looked suitably pained, eyes half closed, head shaking slowly from side to side. "I pulled the girls off the job," he grunted.

"All of them?"

Leo nodded.

"But why?-

"Because "Because they were being conned into going topless." He cupped his hands in front of him the way Sammy Silverman had done earlier. "Blue tits, geddit?"

Claudia's face broke into a smile. "Blue tits? Are you serious?"

Leo threw his head back, raised his hands in front of him. "I don't want to talk about it," he said dismissively. "Let's just say it could easily have ended in tears." His attention strayed to the other side of the room where Lucy's head could just be seen behind the filing cabinet, a look of intense concentration on her face. "If you cat's doing what I think she's doing over there ………"

Claudia span round in her chair in time to see Lucy stepping out from behind the filing cabinet, tail held high. "Naughty girl," she screamed, jumping quickly to her feet and chasing the cat out of the room. She turned to Leo. "If she's done anything I'll clean it up right away."

Leo sighed. "When you've cleaned up after the cat would you call Thatchers estate agency and explain that I don't plan to proceed with the purchase of `Bramble Cottage'." He paused to think for a moment. "Oh, and if he asks to speak to me, tell him I'm out."

"Bad survey?" said Claudia.

"Something like that." Leo slumped back in the chair, hands behind his head. "You never know what you're getting yourself into when you buy a house, especially an old house."

Claudia glanced behind the filing cabinet, smiled nervously and quietly left the room muttering apologies into her hands.

She returned after a few minutes, ready for action, wearing rubber gloves, the smell of disinfectant steaming from a half-filled bucket. Leo felt obliged to help her shuffle the filing cabinet away from the wall, revealing the full extent of Lucy's misdemeanours.

"Does she do that sort of thing at home?" Leo enquired dispassionately as he returned to his desk.

"Never." Claudia knelt down on a folded towel and rubbed at the carpet. "She's completely house trained, always uses her tray."

"Why doesn't she use her tray here then?"

"I don't know." Claudia shrugged. "Cats sometimes like to mark out their territory." She paused to take a closer look at a

149

piece of paper which had been wedged under the corner of the cabinet.

Leo glanced across the room. "I didn't think cats used toilet paper."

"It's a hand written note," Claudia said quietly, rising to her feet.

"Probably slipped down the back," said Leo. "You find all sorts of old rubbish behind filing cabinets."

"I don't think so." Claudia placed the note on Leo's desk. "It's to you and it's dated today."

Leo reached across the desk and slid the note towards him with his index finger. It was brief, written in blue ink. `Friday 13th', it said at the top. `Dear Leo. We need to talk. Contact me.' It was signed `Caroline'.

"I don't understand," said Claudia looking puzzled. "Nobody's been in here today except me."

Leo gave her a reassuring smile. "Don't concern yourself." He screwed up the note and tossed it into the waste bin. "It's probably months old."

He waited for Claudia to finish before making the call to Jonesy. Predictable, Jonesy said. No more than a gentle nudge. But it might be best to explain to Caroline exactly what he'd decided, and soon. Today would be good.

Leo left the office at three o'clock and went straight home.

The decorators had been content with the sound of a pocket-size transistor radio while they worked inside the house, but they apparently needed two on the outside; two much larger ones with long extended aerials, placed strategically either side of the house, each inexplicably tuned to different programmes which collided in jangling discord near the front door. And at the top of a ladder, leaning against the gutter where the smell of burnt paint assaulted the cool afternoon air, the younger of the two men warbled an agonizing tune of his own to the chimney tops.

150

"Sorry about the mess," said the other man who was rubbing-down the window ledges near the garage block. "Must be centuries of god knows what on those facia boards up there."

Leo couldn't think of anything suitable to say. He stood back to admire the progress, nodded in silent agreement, gave the man an appreciative smile and went inside.

"Is five o'clock too early for a very dry martini?" Angela's voice echoed faintly down the hall from the kitchen. From the bar, the sound of Herb Alpert and the Tijuana Brass. "The shaker's charged and in the fridge," she said.

Leo stood in silence for a few moments, dropped his briefcase on a chair just inside the study and slowly made his way towards the open door of the kitchen.

Angela, a tea towel tucked in the front of her jeans as a make-shift apron, turned to greet him. "Steak and salad with a bottle of Mouton Cadet," she said pointing to the garden table, already set for dinner, on the terrace. "And some very smelly Camembert to follow." She opened the fridge door, handed Leo the cocktail shaker and slid two martini glasses across to his side of the kitchen table.

"This is all very nice," said Leo quietly. "A bit unexpected but very nice just the same."

"Say that again." Angela cupped her right hand behind her ear. "Can't hear."

Leo looked concerned. "What's up?"

"Nothing serious," she said. Her face softened into a smile as she carefully removed a small piece of cotton wool from each ear. "It's the only way to listen to Herb Alpert."

"You should be very careful. You might just get to like it."

"About as much chance of that as getting to like Art Deco, which is no chance at all."

Leo tossed a handful of ice cubes into the cocktail shaker. "Three vodkas to one martini I assume," he said, shaking it above his head, in time with the Tijuana Brass.

"Of course." Angela pulled the teat towel from her waistband, quickly dried her hands and reached for one of the glasses. She held it at arm's length for a moment and waited for Leo to do the same. "Happy days," she said, gently clinking glasses. "And many more of them."

"What's been your happiest day so far?" Leo asked, raising his glass to his lips. He quickly turned away in a feeble pretence that the question was unimportant, no more than merely polite conversation, then walked over to the door and fiddled with the lock as if he might be fixing a minor fault with the mechanism.

Angela recognized the charade. "Do you really want to know?" she asked, hoping he'd turn around to face her but knowing his pride wouldn't allow it. Instead he drained the cocktail shaker into his glass without once making eye contact or even looking in her general direction.

"Which day was it?" he said after a pause.

"December 16th."

"December 16th?" he repeated, looking slightly confused. "When?"

"It was nearly ten years ago. 1963."

"So what made it special?"

Angela stared blankly at the kitchen table and shook her head. "Nothing very much. It was just a perfect day that's all."

"Was I a part of it, this perfect day?"

"Oh yes," she whispered. "You were there. We went to the cinema in the Fulham Road. Can't even remember the film, but there was a flurry of snow as we walked home. All the shops ready for Christmas and everyone so happy. That evening has always reminded me of the song, the one that goes *'and we were at peace and the world was alright, once upon a Winter's time'*. Just a magical day."

"It was `The VIP's`," Leo announced proudly. "Richard

Burton and Liz Taylor."

"How clever of you to remember," said Angela.

"Not really. It's about a rich businessman trying to get back his younger wife who's running away with another man."

"How does it end?"

"Not absolutely sure." Leo thought for a moment. "If memory serves, she goes back to her husband."

Angela took hold of his arm and led him out into the garden. "Now that sounds like a perfect ending to me," she said. "The other man obviously didn't deserve her."

"Oh I think the other man deserved her alright," said Leo nodding to himself. "The problem, as I recall, was that he couldn't afford her." He touched her cheek and gently turned her face towards him. "Like Tim Thatcher perhaps, big intentions, small bank balance."

Angela stiffened and pulled away. "I'd better start cooking," she sighed. She flicked her hair casually to one side and strode purposefully back towards the kitchen. "How would you like your steak?"

"As it comes."

"It comes red, raw and bloody," she said sarcastically. "Would you mind telling me how you'd like it cooked?"

"Grilled to perfection," he said, side-stepping an argument.

"One frazzled steak coming up."

Through the half open window Leo watched her move slowly around the kitchen, opening cupboards and drawers, staring into the fridge, searching, looking as if she'd just discovered she might be in the wrong house. The kitchen was unfamiliar territory for Angela who relied on Milly to deal with anything which had the potential to produce a sink full of pots and pans. Grilled steak was well within her limited culinary capabilities but, as she'd said so often, she simply didn't have the rhythm of the kitchen.

A welcome hush descended without warning on the front of

the house when the decorators turned off their radios. One of them appeared at the kitchen door, overalls rolled up under his arm, a canvas bag in his hand. They were finished for the day, he said, going home, and would if be OK if they stacked their ladders at the side of the house. Angela nodded and mumbled something about being careful not to damage the wisteria.

The early evening sun hovered somewhere behind the willow and sent a mottled light across the terrace to the table where Leo fumbled with the flaky remains of a broken cork, wedged firmly in the neck of the wine bottle. He pressed it slowly back into the bottle with the end of a tea spoon and carefully poured two glasses of wine, scooping out the cork residue with his finger.

"Is it warm enough out there?" Angela called from the kitchen. "Maybe we should eat inside after all."

Leo handed her a glass of wine through the open window. "Stick with the original plan," he said softly. "It's a perfect evening, if you overlook the crumbled cork in the wine."

She passed the salad bowl through the window then quickly joined him at the table with two well done steaks and some grilled mushrooms.

Leo pulled back a chair for her to sit down. "Why is eating in the garden always so much more exciting than inside?"

"Because it's not what we usually do. It's a change."

"Is that all it takes to makes life exciting - a change?"

Angela leaned back in the chair, hands resting on the edge of the table. "This isn't leading us back to Tim Thatcher again is it?"

"Not especially, no," said Leo. "I'm just trying to work out what makes people happy." He stared at her for a moment. "What would make you happy right now?"

She sighed and glanced quickly around the garden looking for somewhere to lodge an official complaint. "All these questions," she drawled, finally refocusing on Leo. "First what's been my happiest day so far, then what would make me happy right now. What's this all leading up to?"

Leo covered her hands with his and looked into her eyes. "Just tell me, honestly, what would make you happy right now."

Angela swallowed hard and stared down at the table. "I'd like to be happily married to a happily married man?" she whispered.. "Part of a partnership."

"Well you've certainly been married to a happily married man," said Leo. "The only question seems to be whether you've been happily married as well."

"I don't know." She hesitated for a moment. "Maybe it's more important for me to be loved than to be in love."

"Happy marriages are usually about both parties being in love," Leo said, trickling salt into the shape of a heart on the table. "And usually with each other," he added quickly.

Angela stabbed a fork into her steak and sliced a piece off. "The question is how do you know when you're in love?" she muttered through a mouthful of food. "Isn't it the same as lust?"

"I always thought lust was generally regarded as sinful," said Leo sounding uncharacteristically holy. "Love, on the other hand, is supposed to be the very essence of good."

"What about crimes of passion, people killing for love?"

Leo grinned. "That's uncontrolled lust. Nothing to do with love."

Paddy positioned himself alongside the table, eyes resolutely fixed on Angela's plate, mouth watering, tail slowly wagging in anticipation.

"What do you call that?" said Angela, dropping a small piece of meat to the ground behind her. "Is that lust or passion?"

Leo re-filled the wine glasses. "I'd call it desire. Not a problem unless it becomes an obsession."

"So let's just see if I've got this right." Angela checked her

155

glass for pieces of cork and swilled Mouton Cadet around her mouth like a wine connoisseur. "If I desire a glass of wine, that's OK. If I desire too much wine, it's an obsession, and that's not OK." She took another mouthful of wine. "I suppose addiction is the next stage," she said.

"I suppose so," Leo said quietly.

"Now let's get back to love." She leaned forward across the table, an earnest frown across her brow. "If I lust after a man with a great passion, it's nothing to do with love, right?"

"Wrong. You can lust after someone you *love* with a great passion. That's fine. But lust and passion *alone* are selfish emotions - and love is never selfish."

Angela cupped her chin in her hands and thought for a moment. "Got it. If it's exciting, fun, and ever so slightly naughty, it can't be love."

"I'd say you've managed to confuse the issue slightly." Leo fidgeted on the harsh filigree seat of the wrought iron chair, trying to make himself more comfortable. "When you care about someone else more than yourself, you can be sure it's love."

"Do you honestly believe that?"

"I'm certain of it."

"You'd die for someone you loved?"

Leo cleared his throat. "Who knows? I don't but, I'd like to think so."

"Would you die for me?" Angela stared at him, unblinking, "Would you Leo?"

"The question's academic," he announced quietly but firmly. "Your natural sense of self-preservation wouldn't let you within a mile of mortal danger."

Angela let out a long, deep sigh and searched Leo's face for a straightforward, uncomplicated 'yes' or `no' answer but the bland expression gave nothing away. She decided the answer was probably `no'. Who cared anyway?

156

The second bottle of wine surrendered its cork without a struggle and disappeared with equal ease, making way for a third which was opened, without hesitation and with few misgivings, to accompany the cheese.

"Are you trying to get me tipsy?" Angela asked, squinting with one eye through a half empty wine glass. "It certainly feels like it."

"A few glasses of wine won't do you any harm," said Leo. "Best thing for a good night's sleep."

"What if I just want a good night, without the sleep bit?" Angela slid a hand through her hair and fluffed it out to one side. "What if I'd like to stay awake half the night, the way we used to?"

"That was ten years ago," Leo said wearily. "When we didn't have separate bedrooms."

Angela scowled then playfully stuck out her tongue like a small child and rose unsteadily to her feet. "Stay exactly where you are," she ordered, wagging her finger under his nose. She thought for a second, picked up a steak knife and stepped back along the terrace, towards the side of the house where she disappeared from view.

Leo poured himself another glass of wine and waited. "What are you doing?" he called out after a short while.

"Wait and see." She returned carrying a single red rose and sucking her finger."

"Have you cut yourself?"

"The rose attacked me," she said, laying it on the table in front of him. "It's for you - an invitation to join me in the matrimonial bedroom after dinner where I am making arrangements for all night lust."

Leo gently picked up the rose and twiddled it under his nose. "Its beautiful," he said. "Thank you."

"Never mind the rose, what about the RSVP?" she snapped, flopping down on the chair and reaching for her glass. "Are you coming to my orgy or not?"

"But of course." Leo leaned across the table and kissed her on the cheek. "What red-blooded man could refuse such an invitation?"

"But are you as red-blooded as me?" Angela squeezed a small droplet of blood to the tip of her finger and stared at it for a moment then reached for the rose, took hold of his hand, and gently pricked his finger with the thorny stem. "Blood brothers," she declared, pressing their two fingers together.

"Can a man and a woman be blood brothers?" Leo asked dabbing his finger with a paper serviette. "Shouldn't two people on their way to an orgy be blood partners or something?"

"If you like. Anyway the dress code is informal," she said in her most superior voice. "Pyjamas will not be worn. Anyone found with them on will be evicted from the orgy."

Leo smiled. "Bad form not to heed a rigid dress code." He emptied his glass and began collecting up the plates. "I assume your orgy is after we've done the washing-up?"

"Definitely not. The dishes can wait until tomorrow."

He reached for her hand as she turned to leave the table. "You go ahead," he said quietly. "I've got something I need to do. Business."

She turned, eyes blinking rapidly setting the world back into focus. "One of your marathon 'phone calls to god knows where, is it?"

"Something like that," he murmured. "It could take a while."

"Well don't be too long. I think I may be ever so slightly squiffy and I'd hate to sleep through my own orgy."

Angela swaggered playfully into the house, pausing to wiggle her bottom for her one man audience and turning three or four times to wave before disappearing into the hall.

"Oh, and by the way," she called from the foot of the stairs, "I think you should probably know that maybe I possibly love you a bit. Is that alright?"

"It's very possibly probably fine - maybe." Leo leaned back in the chair, legs crossed, and giggled to himself. He wasn't absolutely sure why nor did he care.

The night air, suddenly quite chill with a dampness that hinted at the onset of autumn, still carried a trace of the fading scent of summer, now cloaked by the unmistakable sour smell of fallen apples. Leo sniffed the dank, misty odour of decay which drifted across the grass, already wet with dew, and sent an involuntary shiver through his body. It reminded him of his childhood, the end of the summer holidays and the start of a new autumn term, surely the most depressing time of the year.

Arms briskly rubbed for warmth, back stretched and straightened, legs still slightly stiff, Leo glanced up at a clear, cold sky, a half moon, low in the trees, over to the south. Time to talk to Caroline, sort things out, once and for all.

Paddy uncurled himself from under the table and followed Leo into the house, then trotted upstairs to a vantage point on the landing and watched him pour a large brandy before closing the lounge door behind him. He settled himself on the couch and stared at the reflection in the mosaic fireplace; a living jigsaw puzzle of tiny mirrored pieces, all neatly slotted together to create the slightly irregular picture of Leo Gannesh reclining with a drink.

"Why, I wonder," he whispered to the ceiling, "do I feel like a cheat?" He stretched his arms out across the back of the couch and allowed his eyes to slowly close. "The simple answer is that I am a cheat. I've got a wife who maybe possibly loves me a bit but who's completely in the dark about my other woman - albeit a woman who, for the moment at least, doesn't exist." He raised his head wearily. "You sir," he said pointing at his jigsaw reflection. "You are definitely a bloody cheat of the first order."

Leo leaned forward, elbows on knees, and swirled the

brandy around in the glass. "So where the hell are you Caroline? I've got some important things to tell you." He looked around the room, half expecting to see her leaning casually against the window, wearing the silky white dress. But there was nothing.

Across the garden, barely visible behind the trees, the moon glimmered through a pale yellow haze, like a candle flickering in a distant window. Leo stared hard, closed his eyes and tried to focus his thoughts on Caroline. If he was totally honest it was difficult to conjure-up a clear picture of the lightly tanned face, the auburn hair, the elfin features, not completely anyway. The vision was fading but the feeling inside was still as strong, every bit as clear and painful, just as painful as ever. The undeniable truth was that life without Caroline would seem pointless, empty, a void in time. Limbo in fact. But he'd resigned himself to a dull, colourless future and would try to make the best of it, rebuild some sort of life with Angela, possibly even enjoy it. Why not? It didn't really matter. Caroline's magic would live inside him until it was time to go, to start again with her, the next time. It was a comforting thought and he would cling to it.

Through half open eyes Leo watched a new mist creep across the tops of the trees, quickly blotting out the moon and shrouding the garden in murky grey. Swirling fog, suddenly, unaccountably from nowhere, drifting across the garden. And through the window the acrid smell of smoke, a bonfire possibly, one of the neighbours burning garden waste, foul smelling rubbish, under cover of darkness. Inconsiderate bastards.

Leo rose slowly to his feet, placed the empty brandy glass on top of the fire place and stood, arms folded, looking out of the widow. "What happens now Caroline?" he sighed, staring into the dark. "How do I focus on a moon that isn't there?" In a moment he turned his back on the night and started towards the door - and the carpet of smoke which rolled out from under it, across the floor towards him. In the hall a choking fog, the smell of burning; fire somewhere in the house.

A tea towel from the kitchen, soaked in water, across the mouth. Wasn't that what they always said? No time to think. Leo ran to the front door, calling out, turning on lights. Then outside where flames curled out from under the eaves and danced across the roof tiles, upwards to the sky; smoke surging across the drive towards the garage block; Paddy barking, panting, on the lawn.

And Angela. Still upstairs, perhaps asleep. Leo called out, tightened the towel across his mouth and went back into the house, over to the stairs, one foot on the bottom step. He called out again, louder this time. Stupid. Lungs filled with stinging smoke and the crackle of burning wood the only response.

The lights flickered for an instant and then darkness on the stairs. On the landing, from beyond the bedroom doors, an amber glow penetrated the dense grey fog and above, stabbing through the ceiling like a crazed army of looters, angry daggers of flame sent plaster and wood crashing to the floor.

Leo reached out to the figure slumped, unmoving, just below the landing at the turn of the stairs; Angela, still conscious, still breathing, her eyes filled with terror, grabbing blindly at his arm. She slipped back against the wall, hands to her throat, choking, coughing.

Hot acrid smoke, now everywhere, flooding the house, billowing out into the darkness. No more time. Each fiery intake of breath tearing into the lungs like blazing talons. He threw his arms around her waist, hands clasped firmly together, and lurched backwards down the stairs, dragging, pulling, slowly to the door and bright lights on the other side, flashing across the front of the house.

The ornate ceiling collapsed in crumbling slabs, like decorative icing from a huge cake, showering the hall with rubble, sending Leo crashing back against the banister. For a fleeting moment he stood perfectly still, totally resolved, unhurried, then teeth clenched, eyes narrowed against the blinding smoke, he stumbled forward pushing Angela headlong across the hall towards the porch and the cool night air.

A sharp pain across his back, quickly gone, and then a welcoming calm, pleasantly numb. Outside, a ladder reaching for the heavens from a rumbling, vibrating fire engine, the light from inside the ambulance, rear doors wide open and men in uniforms comforting Angela on the edge of the lawn, eyes wide open, one hand reaching out towards the house. Bright red blankets, oxygen masks, people in control, everything as it should be. Safe surely?

Leo stared up at the figure on the ladder as it moved closer to the house and formed a triangle with the roof, water gushing from a long brass nozzle into the smoke, pounding against the rafters.

He cursed the decorators and their blow torches, scorched wood along the eaves, the dry fabric of the roof smouldering through the evening. Stupid, mindless bastards.

Along the drive, closer to the lawn, men with helmets, a stretcher. Someone covered in a red blanket, hidden, motionless. Paddy anxious, barking. Angela, head buried in her hands.

But nothing to be done. All perfectly OK. No sadness, please, no tears. I was and will be again. It's sure, certain, the way of things.

Brighter than before, higher in the sky, a dazzling white light, soothing, peaceful, the way back beckoning from the blurred edges of darkness.

And Caroline's voice on the wind beyond the trees.

"It's time my darling Leo."

But of course. Understood.   Everything just as it should be. No more words. Peace.

Leo Gannesh took a last lingering look towards 'Pelham Green Farm House' then turned away with a hopeful heart.

He didn't look back.